ON THE CLOCK

Praises for *On The Clock*

On The Clock is a page turner you do not want to miss! This is a behind the scenes story at what it takes for Adam, a young quarterback and his country music star father to follow and pursue their own scary, yet incredible God-given dreams!

—**Mark Batterson**, *New York Times* Best-Selling author of *The Circle Maker*, Lead Pastor of National Community Church

Everybody gets to see what happens when the lights are on and the camera is rolling. Many times, the real story is what happens in private where there are no lights and camera. *On The Clock* is your backstage pass into the lives of a country music star dad (Peter Alford) and his superstar quarterback son (Adam Alford). In this book, you will see what happens off camera that sets the stage for what could be the best sports story of the year!

—**Heather Cox**, NBC Sports

Life is short. Discovering what matters most and acting on it changes everything! *On The Clock* is a remarkable story of a dad and his son working their way through the ups and downs of life and in the process discovering what's most important—relationships! It is the perfect book for anyone who has ever been the underdog in life.

—**Sean Covey**, *New York Times* Best-Selling author of *The 4 Disciplines of Execution* and *The 7 Habits of Highly Effective Teens*

As you turn the pages of this delightful book, you'll realize there is more than an enjoyable story here! You'll learn leadership and personal growth principles along with the main character, Adam Alford, as you follow the ups and downs of his impassioned pursuit towards his purpose in life. Tim and Bruce have combined their talents and expertise in *On*

The Clock and the end result will inspire you to make use of your own God-given talents in achieving your personal purpose in life as well!

—**Holly Duncan**, Leadership Director—Southlands Christian
Schools, Author of *Listen, My Son; There are Plans for You*

In life, every day is game day! There are days when the score is made public, and days when there are only private victories or challenges… but in the end, EVERY DAY COUNTS! In this book, Tim and Bruce share a captivating story about a rising star quarterback and his country music star dad who face devastating storms in life. In the midst of their storms, they discover they control the narrative best by anchoring in their core values. By applying the principles written in this book, you can discover how to Win the Day, every day!

—**Coach Hugh Freeze**, Head Football Coach,
The University of Mississippi

Our days are numbered. In this exciting and suspenseful book, Tim and Bruce will show you how to make them all count. I highly recommend *On The Clock*.

—**Robert D. Smith**, Author of *20,000 Days and Counting*

In football and life, you can't just expect something good is going to fall in your lap. You have to go for it. You have to throw the ball downfield. In *On The Clock*, Tim and Bruce take you behind the scenes of two very different, and yet somewhat similar, worlds of the NFL and country music. In this intriguing book, while being caught up in the story of an aspiring quarterback and his country music star dad, you will learn principles of success you can use in your own life.

—**Jerry Reese**, Senior Vice President and General Manager
New York Football Giants, Winner of Super Bowls XLII & XLVI

I highly recommend this book! *On The Clock* is an incredible story that will pull you behind the scenes of the NFL and country music, and teach you principles of success you can use today. As I wrote in The Amos Paradigm, the promise of Amos 9:13 offers a new paradigm of faith and expectation, where old disappointments give way to new realities of expedience and abundant fruitfulness. That's what you find in this story of a rising star quarterback and his singer-songwriter dad.

—*Dr. Tim Hill*, General Overseer, the Church of God

On The Clock combines inspirational and thought-provoking messages applicable to pursuing one's passion and purpose in life, along with the insight of knowing that once those are visible, it is not the finish line, it is just the beginning.

—**Mark Brunell**, Jacksonville Jaguar Hall of Fame Quarterback and former ESPN Analyst, Head Coach at the Episcopal School of Jacksonville

On The Clock is about more than country music and football, it's about winning the game of life the right way. It's about more than a relationship between a son and his dad, it's about going for it and making it when the rest of the world seems to be against you. This is an inspiring, must read!

—**Akbar GbajaBiamila**, Analyst—NFL Network, Co-host—American Ninja Warrior

This is more than a football story, told by insiders, but a life-affirming tribute to a fascinating character—someone we can all cheer for. We'd all be elbowing for position to land the first interview with Adam Alford!

—**Sam Farmer**, *Los Angeles Times*

I know what it's like to be in the fight of your life right at the point where your biggest dreams are coming true. In *On The Clock*, Bruce and Tim invite you behind the curtains of a young man's life to show you how he fought through adversity in hope of seeing his dream come true. You can't always count on life—or football games—to go as you expect. The message in this book inspires you to focus on the process, do the work, take it one day at a time, and stick to it as you pursue your dreams.

—**Coach Chuck Pagano**, Head Coach—Indianapolis Colts

This book combines suspense with inside information on the NFL draft process. It helped me think about my unique personal purpose in life.

—**Pat Davidson**, Educator & Academic Specialist

On The Clock is an inspirational, lesson-laden story that gives an inside look at Adam Alford's roller coaster journey, from childhood to the NFL, as he searches for his passion and purpose in life. You don't have to be a football fan to enjoy the story. I highly recommend it.

—**Steve Mariucci**, NFL Network, Former NFL Head Coach

On The Clock is a compelling story Bruce and Tim built around a theme that will help you reach higher and accomplish more. As you read the story of quarterback, Adam Alford, and his country music star dad, Peter, you will find yourself not only turning the page to see what happens next, but turning the page to see how you can apply what you have read in your own life.

—**Kabeer Gbaja-Biamila**, Green Bay Packers
Hall of Fame—Defensive End

Enjoyed every page of *On The Clock* and couldn't wait to read what was coming next. In a culture filled with broken relationships, refreshing to see what can transpire when love, commitment and self-sacrifice are embedded in a father/son relationship. Story of hope through adversity and cream rising to the top.

—**Mark Boyer**, Vice President of Field Ministry, Western Region, Fellowship of Christian Athletes

If you've ever wondered what it takes to be a champion, read this book! *On The Clock* is an amazing story that gives you a front row seat and behind the scenes peak at what it takes to win.

—**Allyson Felix**, Track & Field Olympic Multi-Gold Medal Winner and World Champion

On The Clock takes you on a journey through the fire with country music star Peter Alford and his quarterback son, Adam. You don't want to miss any part of this unpredictable ride!

—**Jason Crabb**, Grammy Winner

The opening chapters of *On The Clock* are like watching Ben Roethlisberger fighting to win his third Super Bowl with five seconds left on the clock. He chucks up a Hail Mary into the air towards Antonio Brown who is leaping above three defenders in the corner of the end zone. It puts you on the edge of your seat, palms sweating, and heart racing as you read through the unfathomable events that kick off this book. Does he make the catch? Does Adam Alford fight through the unimaginable barriers piled in front of him like the Steel Curtain from the days of old? Can he quarterback sneak his way to being the NFL quarterback he always dreamed he'd be? One can only hope he captures the trophy like he captures your heart!

—**Carlee Roethlisberger**, Two Sport Athlete— University of Oklahoma / Beach Volleyball Pro

ON THE
CLOCK

TIM ENOCHS &
BRUCE TOLLNER

NEW YORK

NASHVILLE   MELBOURNE

ON THE CLOCK

Published in New York, New York, by Morgan James Publishing. Morgan James and The Entrepreneurial Publisher are trademarks of Morgan James, LLC. www.MorganJamesPublishing.com

The Morgan James Speakers Group can bring authors to your live event. For more information or to book an event visit The Morgan James Speakers Group at www.TheMorganJamesSpeakersGroup.com.

ISBN 978-1-68350-040-7 paperback
ISBN 978-1-68350-041-4 eBook
ISBN 978-1-68350-042-1 hardcover
Library of Congress Control Number:
2016905885

Cover Design by:
Rachel Lopez
www.r2cdesign.com

Interior Design by:
Bonnie Bushman
The Whole Caboodle Graphic Design

Shelfie

A **free** eBook edition is available
with the purchase of this print book.

CLEARLY PRINT YOUR NAME ABOVE IN UPPER CASE
Instructions to claim your free eBook edition:
1. Download the Shelfie app for Android or iOS
2. Write your name in **UPPER CASE** above
3. Use the Shelfie app to submit a photo
4. Download your eBook to any device

In an effort to support local communities, raise awareness and funds, Morgan James Publishing donates a percentage of all book sales for the life of each book to Habitat for Humanity Peninsula and Greater Williamsburg.

Get involved today! Visit
www.MorganJamesBuilds.com

PROLOGUE

Less than 24 hours ago, I officially accepted an offer that will allow me to live out my lifelong dream. With the stroke of a pen, I made a commitment that not only changes my life right now, but for years to come. Saying this opportunity was a game changer for me would be an understatement.

And it has all happened so fast. Yesterday was a complete blur; it was a day I had waited my whole life to arrive. But now I want to slow down, think about what's happened this past year, and begin to process it all. And I'll have a little help. Today, I'm sitting in my agent's office, about to share my story with a reporter who will make it known to the world. It's a story of moments I'm proud of as well as ones I'm hesitant to share with anyone.

Why am I doing it?

Two reasons. Most of all, I want my story to inspire all the underdogs, people who, like me, may have had challenges and who may be about to give up on their dreams. My dream was almost taken from me, mainly because of some mistakes I made. There were times I almost gave up. But ultimately I pushed through and kept working, hoping and trusting for the best. So I don't want anyone to give up on their dreams, no matter how impossible or far away they may seem. I want my story to help them hang on, to keep fighting until they win.

I also want to inspire achievers to be intentional about having uncommon influence on others. This is the kind of unique personal influence that changes the trajectory of another person's life. I want people to realize how they can have uncommon influence that will help others achieve their dreams. I wasn't alone in my quest to live out my dream. As you will see, I've had several people who have had that kind of uncommon influence on me. Now I want to pass it along to others who need a spark of hope. Against all odds, your dreams can come true—*if* you're willing to fight those odds and to keep the faith.

If I seem nervous, it's because what I'm about to share is very personal. Some of it may seem unbelievable. If it hadn't happened to me, I'm not sure I would believe it myself. Some of my story has been all-too-well reported by sports writers and others on social media, while some parts have never been revealed to anyone.

Most people would say I'm living the dream—myself included. I just signed a contract that instantly made me a multi-millionaire. I'm about to start a job doing what I've always dreamed of doing.

But it's been a long hard journey getting here.

I wouldn't say any of it has been easy.

And the journey is not over yet.

CHAPTER 1

"**W**hen I grow up, I'm going to be an NFL quarterback!"

I remember so clearly the way my mom and dad smiled at my certainty. Mom was folding my clothes, along with Dad's, for our trip when she had looked over at me. She said, "Adam, you're the spitting image of your dad, just a younger version. I think the only difference is you're more interested in football than singing."

That's when I had set the record straight about my career ambitions. Dad had walked in the room just in time to hear me and said, "I like football, too, buddy, but I'd rather see you singing to pretty girls than tackled by big, ugly guys!"

We all laughed as Mom kept packing. She was not only collecting my stuff for the trip, but she packed Dad's, too. She knew if it were up to him, he would either buy new clothes at every tour stop or wear the same thing he had on for the next 27 days. Without Mom, he would have stepped on that tour bus without packing anything but his guitar.

"Here you go, boys. You're all packed up and ready to go." She zipped the suitcase, and I ran over to help her lift it from the bed. Then it was time to go.

I'll never forget reaching out and giving my mom a big hug right then. We both held on a little tighter and a little longer than usual.

"Mom, you're the best. I wish you could go with us, but I understand you need to stay here to help Grandma take care of Grandpa."

"I wish I could go too, buddy," she said. "But I will catch up with you guys in Louisville. Grandpa should be okay by then and Jake's wife, Sandy, is going to come to Louisville with me."

"Okay, Mom—but I'm still going to really miss you."

+ + +

I grew up with an amazing family. Mom and Dad were so close and loved each other with a love that's rarely seen today. They met at a little church in the mountains. Mom had come from Oklahoma to visit her sister in Tennessee. Dad said he noticed how beautiful Mom was right away with her olive skin, brown eyes, and dark hair. As a strong woman of Polynesian descent, she was used to attracting attention. But she noticed Dad too, even though as he says he's "just an average Joe." They must have fallen in love pretty quickly because she never went back to Oklahoma. Her parents, my Grandma and Grandpa, moved here to Inspiration.

Inspiration is my hometown just northeast of Chattanooga, nestled right in between the Great Smoky Mountains and the Appalachians. It was a great place to grow up. We didn't have a lot of stuff, but I never felt poor.

My dad worked whatever jobs he had to work in order to pay the bills, but what he loved the most was writing songs and playing his guitar. He'd play local bars on most Friday and Saturday nights and then lead the worship band at church on Sunday mornings. He also played farmer's markets and county fairs, really anywhere they'd let him.

Then he got noticed by a talent scout and signed to a major label. When I was ten, my dad charted his first single as a rising singer-songwriter on the country music scene. He was about to leave with his band to go on tour to promote his new album, which included his new #1 Billboard Country hit, "These Ain't Raindrops." At long last his dream was coming true, and Mom and I couldn't have been happier.

Because I was out of school for spring break, I convinced Dad to take me with him on the tour bus for a few days. Mom agreed and planned to meet us on the third stop of the tour and then bring me home. The first show was planned for Richmond, Virginia, then Charlotte, North Carolina, and back through Louisville, Kentucky, where Mom was going to meet us.

I was so excited about going on tour with Dad. I'll never forget that day, a Friday at the end of March. It had been really cloudy and windy all day. I'd heard Grandpa and his friends talk about the way, if March came in like a lamb, it would go out like a lion. If you've ever lived in the South, you know what that means. When the weather is clear and calm at the beginning of March, it will be stormy at the end. It sure seemed so that year.

Dad and I had been to the store to pick up some last minute supplies for the trip. We were planning to leave at 4:00 the next morning so Dad and the band could get to Richmond in time for setup and sound check for the Saturday night show. As usual, driving home my dad had the sound cranked up on the radio. Foreigner's classic "Feels Like the First Time" was blaring, and my dad was using the steering wheel as a drum set while singing at the top of his lungs, "I would climb any mountain..."

Out of nowhere, as my dad continued to sing, the song was replaced by a piercing alarm:

"This is an alert of the Emergency Weather Service. The National Weather Service in Chattanooga, Tennessee, has issued a severe thunderstorm watch in effect for the entire region of Southeast Tennessee...Including frequent to excessive lightning... gusty winds from 45 to 55 miles per hour... up to golf ball-sized hail... until 7:30 AM EST Saturday. At least two storm systems will pass through the region during the night, dumping up to an inch of rain each hour. Flash flooding is possible. Conditions are favorable for the formation of a tornado. Residents in the area should remain on the alert for additional information and possible warnings."

The words of the automated voice cut through our good mood.

Dad turned the radio off and called my mom right away; we both knew she had always been terrified of thunderstorms. She would occasionally describe the tornado that ravaged her hometown in Oklahoma and killed three people when she was nine years old. Understandably, she had always been afraid of storms and the destruction they could bring.

"Went to voicemail," Dad said to me before leaving his message. "Emily, we just heard the weather advisory—call me."

"She's probably talking to Grandma," I said and he nodded.

Then Dad noticed he'd missed a call from Jake, his road manager, and hit the call button to call him back. Jake answered on the first ring and sounded like he'd just run a marathon.

"Have you heard the news?"

"About the storm coming in?" Dad said. "Yeah, we just heard it on the radio. I tried calling Emily but didn't get her—'cause you know how much she hates storms."

"She's not the only one—you know what this means don't you?"

"Yeah, it means it might be raining when we start out in the morning, and it probably means Emily won't want me to leave that early."

"Well too bad—we need to get out of Dodge now!" Jake exclaimed.

"*Now?*" my dad asked.

"Yes, right now. I don't think you want to be on the road riding in a bus in the middle of a major thunderstorm, do you?"

"Well, not if I have a choice."

Jake continued, "Then we need to get a head start on the storm and leave now. I would much rather be ahead of it as much as we can. If we don't leave now, we could be caught in the middle of it as it passes through. The last thing we need is for some storm to make us cancel the first night of our tour just because we didn't leave town when we could."

"I don't know…let me talk to Emily."

Dad was always concerned about Mom. Even though she's a strong lady, he liked protecting her as much as he could.

"Emily will just have to understand," Jake said. "I'm sure she'll be on board."

Dad chuckled. "Yeah, we'll see about that. Let me call you back. I'm turning in the driveway right now. Maybe I can get her to stay with her parents tonight."

"We don't have a choice, Peter," Jake sighed. "The bus will be packed and at your house to pick you and Adam up at eight tonight. So be ready!"

We turned into the driveway, and sure enough, Mom was on the porch talking on her cell phone and looking up at the sky. As soon as she saw us, she ended her call and ran to meet us.

"Peter, I'm so glad you are home. Have you heard what's coming?"

"Yeah, there's a big storm coming in like a lion!" I said.

Dad glanced at me.

"Yeah, we heard, babe," he said, pulling Mom in close to him. "But it's only a forecast you know. The weather changes like… well… you know… the weather!"

Mom didn't laugh at his attempt at a joke. "Yeah, but they are making this storm sound bad!"

"Emily, since when has a weather forecast for storms not sounded bad to you?"

"Peter..."

"I know," Dad said with an understanding smile.

We headed into the house, and Mom seemed to relax, at least for a moment. She said, "I'm just glad you aren't leaving until the morning. It should all pass by then."

"Well, about that..." Dad began but couldn't finish.

"What do you mean, 'about that'?"

"Jake called, and...well, we were already going to leave pretty early anyway."

Mom started getting that fearful look in her eyes again. "What do you mean, 'were', and 'anyway'? You aren't leaving tonight are you?"

Dad hesitated.

"*You are, aren't you?*"

"Jake thinks we need to beat the storm and—"

"*Beat the storm?* So you do believe it will storm tonight don't you?" She was about to cry.

Dad hesitated again, searching for the right words to say. They had left me in the kitchen to get a snack, but I could still hear their conversation.

"Emily, it's going to be okay. It's probably just going to be a lot of rain, and Jake doesn't want us to be late for setup and sound check for our first night. You know this tour is huge for us—for my career, for our family, for all of us. Why don't you just stay at your mom and dad's tonight? After all, they have that bedroom down in the basement. You and Adam can sleep down there and never even hear a storm if it comes through."

I was ready to rush in and protest, but Mom was already ahead of me.

"Don't forget Adam is going with you and I am picking him up in Louisville."

"I didn't mean to say that. I know Adam is going. You know I want Adam to be with me on this trip—and I want you to be with us, too."

"You know I would if I could," she said. "But with my dad's outpatient surgery on his shoulder tomorrow, I need to stay and help Mom take care of him."

"Emily, you know I love your mom and dad and completely understand why you can't be with us on tour. But I do have to go, and we need to leave tonight. Yes, a little storm will probably come through, and it would be better for us to be ahead of it instead of risk missing our opening night. You'll be safe with your folks, and we'll be safely ahead of the storm and almost to Richmond when you wake up in the morning. It's all going to be okay."

Mom visibly relaxed and fell into Dad's arms. He always had a way of saying the right thing at the right time, especially when he felt like he was in a tight spot.

"You're right, honey," she said. "I'll call Mom and let her know I'm staying over there tonight. Lord knows, I'd rather be in their basement than here on top of this hill by myself in the middle of a storm."

"Great. You call your mom, get Adam ready, and I'll tell Jake we'll be ready to leave by eight."

"*Eight?*"

"Emily…"

"Okay, right—eight it is."

+ + +

Unknown to Mom and Dad, weather forecasters only became more and more concerned about the night ahead. The approaching line of storms was beginning to intensify as the hot surface air collided with the cooler air being pumped in with the front. Storm chasers were positioning themselves in the area as the data poured in, pinpointing our area as the center of storm activity over the next several hours.

Mom called Grandma and let her know Dad and I were leaving early to beat the rain, and that she was coming over for the night. Grandma was glad she was coming. She had been watching the weather reports all afternoon and noticed the forecasters had intensified their warnings for the night. She, too, had been very concerned about storms over the years. Her best friend's husband had been killed in that tornado all those years ago when Mom was a girl. But Grandma had such a strong faith—she always remained calm no matter what happened. I'll always remember how Grandma—and Grandpa, too—loved me and prayed for me and our family all the time.

Finally, the time came to say our goodbyes. Dad hugged Mom close to his chest and said, "You really are the best. I don't know what I'd do without you. I think I'll write a song about Louisville, you know, like Larry Gatlin wrote about Houston. Something like 'Louisville means I'm one day closer to you.'"

They both laughed and Mom said, "You better think about that a little more before you write it, sweetheart. Louisville doesn't mean you're one day closer to me—Louisville means we're together again. I'll be there waiting before you, Adam, and the band get there."

Dad winked at mom.

"Even better! See what I mean? 'Louisville means we're together again'—that's perfect. I don't know what I would do without you. You're a great mom, a great wife, a great cook, you're beautiful, *and* you're a poet! I'm the most blessed man alive, and…"

Mom pulled back and interrupted Dad while he was piling it on. "Okay, I get it. This is the time you want me to say you're a great dad, a great husband, a great singer-songwriter…"

"If the two of you are my parents," I said, "then I must be Adam Alford, the greatest quarterback on earth."

We all laughed and shared a tight group hug, our family tradition anytime any of us were going to be away for long. Then after a quick kiss from Dad and another hug from me, Mom got in her car and drove off to Grandma and Grandpa's house. As Dad and I were gathering our bags to get on the waiting bus, his phone rang. It was Mom.

"I forgot, Mom wanted me to tell you that she and Grandpa love you two so much, and she will be praying for you guys on the tour. You know, next to Adam and me, she and Dad are your biggest fans."

Dad said, "I know. Tell them we love them too."

"Alright, I'll be waiting for you in Louisville."

"And I'll start writing that song. Next time I see you, I'll play it for you!"

CHAPTER 2

Dad and I got on the bus with Jake and the band. Everyone was talking about the impending storm system moving through, and the fact that they were glad we were getting out of town before it hit. But I was still worried and asked, "Dad, is Mom really going to be okay?"

Always reassuring, he answered, "Of course, buddy. She'll be fine. She'll be down in that basement bedroom at Grandma and Grandpa's— why it's probably the safest place in Inspiration! We'll see her in Louisville in a couple of days. So don't you worry about a thing."

That made me smile. Dad hugged me and told me to go ahead and get in my bunk on the bus and get some sleep because he needed me to help with setup the next day. He always had a way of making me feel special and needed. As I started back to my bunk, I turned around and looked at him one more time.

"Are you sure Mom will be okay, Dad?"

"I am as sure of that as I am of anything in this world, buddy."

That was all I needed to hear.

"Good night, Dad."

"Good night, buddy."

As I headed toward my bunk at the back of the bus, I could hear footsteps right behind me.

Dad said, "You didn't think I was going to let you tuck yourself into bed did you?"

"Well, I am getting kinda old for it…"

"What? You don't want your old dad tucking you in every night?" And then he tried to tickle me as I lunged into my bunk. As I tried to stop laughing uncontrollably, I grabbed my old football, which I took everywhere with me, and climbed under the covers.

"Okay, big guy," he said. "Time to settle down." He tucked me in and tried to take the football, but I held tight. "Are you sure you don't want to trade that old football for a guitar?"

"I'm sure, Dad. You'll see one day. I am going to be a big football star. I'll win more Super Bowls than any quarterback ever has before!"

"You're already a star to me, buddy," Dad said with a smile. "Good night, Double A."

Double A was Dad's nickname for me, claiming my initials also stood for "All-American" as well as Adam Alford. He wanted me to know I could be a star in anything I wanted to do. He wanted me to know that he believed in me no matter what.

After tucking me into my bunk, dad went back toward the front of the bus where the band members and Jake were watching TV. The record label provided us with an amazing bus loaded with everything you could want while on tour, even satellite TV. The only thing we didn't have with us was Mom.

I was pretty tired and went right to sleep. But something woke me up. It was the guys in the front of the bus. I opened the curtain of the bunk a little and leaned out so I could hear better. Listening to bits and pieces of the talk up front, I could tell something was going on which concerned them all.

They were watching a special news report about the line of storms headed toward home.

Multiple tornadoes had been reported with this first line of storms, and several homes in their path had been damaged. I could tell Stanley, the bass guitarist, was pretty nervous about the situation. His wife, Katie, was pregnant with their first child with only a few weeks to go. I heard him make a call to be sure she was okay, but she must have been asleep because it sounded like she gave him a hard time for waking her up.

George, the drummer, also called his wife, Kim, to check on her. She was fine. She had been awake watching the reports but told George that it looked like most of the bad stuff was going to the north of them. She thought they were just going to get a lot of rain and some wind the rest of the night. Jonathan, the keyboardist, was single and his parents lived down in Florida. The other band members kidded him about having too many girlfriends to call.

Then I heard my Dad's voice calling Mom and putting her on speaker. She said she'd just arrived at Grandma and Grandpa's house after picking up batteries and some additional groceries Grandma asked her to pick up on her way.

"You should have seen the lines of people," she said. "It looked like just about everybody in town needed milk and bread, or batteries and flashlights. The guy in front of me had at least ten packs of toilet paper. He must think this storm is going to last a while."

"Or else he's afraid the storm might scare the you-know-what out of him. I'll have to remember to stock up next time another storm comes through." Mom said something I couldn't hear then, and everybody in the front of the bus laughed.

Dad took her off speaker then, and they talked for a while longer before he wrapped up the call. At that point I started to feel more comfortable about the storm situation. Maybe nothing was going to happen after all.

By the time Dad got off the phone with Mom, the other guys in the band started playing cards to pass the time. Although they were concerned about the people hit by the storm to the north of where we lived, they seemed comforted by the knowledge that this first wave appeared to be missing Inspiration. I eventually fell asleep.

+ + +

I don't know how long I was asleep before I heard a commotion. The first voice I heard was Dewayne's, the bus driver my dad had insisted on for this tour. They had known each other since Dad was a student singing in Campus Choir at Lee University many years ago. Dewayne had been the driver and handyman at the university until he'd recently retired. Everybody loved Dewayne.

It was hard to hear exactly what he was saying, but clearly something was wrong. The voice of his wife Sally came through in static bursts—he must've had her on speaker—and I heard "...something horrible... Inspiration...tornado...." My heart drummed inside my chest and I felt a shiver down my back.

George called Kim, and she let him know a big tornado had just hit near Inspiration. She was okay but said the big wooden fence in their backyard had been destroyed. Stanley got Katie on the line, and she said she was shaken up but otherwise okay. She'd heard the tornado pass through less than a mile away, though. She said it sounded like a freight train. Jonathan talked to a buddy of his at one of the clubs near Cleveland, Tennessee, which had missed the storm entirely. Dad's manager, Jake, talked to his wife and she was fine.

At some point as everyone was comparing notes, Dad woke up and asked what was going on. Everybody started talking at once, so he tried to calm them down and get the facts straight. I sat on the edge of my bunk and just listened. After hearing everyone's report, dad grabbed his phone from the table where he'd left it charging before he went to bed. There were no missed calls, no texts, NOTHING from Mom or her parents.

I went to stand next to him, and he wrapped an arm around my shoulder as he cradled the phone. I was close enough beside him to hear it ringing. But then all we could hear was a fast busy signal. He dialed again and got the same thing.

He tried Grandma's and Grandpa's cell numbers and got the same fast busy signals for both. He tried mom's phone again with no luck.

Stanley said, "Maybe the tower is down, or the lines are jammed."

"Mom's fine, right?" I said and pulled away. "Dad, you promised me she would be fine."

Dad stared at the floor wishing he had the right words to say. "Buddy, I'm as worried as you are. But I need you to head back to your bunk and try to sleep. I'll let you know as soon as I talk to your mom."

Jonathan took me by the arm and said, "Come on, Double A. Superstar quarterbacks need their sleep." He took me back to my bunk, tucked me in, and turned some music on the speakers installed in every bunk. He set the system to something soothing, classical, I think. I was so worried about Mom that I couldn't imagine going back to sleep. I just tossed and turned. The bus was moving again, rocking back and forth because of the wind. I overheard someone say we were on our way back to Inspiration.

I got up, wrapped myself in the blanket from my bunk, and went looking for Dad. I followed the sound of his voice to the back lounge area where we had a small fridge, microwave, and lots of snacks. I snuggled in close to Dad's shoulder as he continued talking on his cell to Rick, his booking agent.

"So what's going on back there now?"

Rick hesitated. "Peter, I'm not exactly sure…but something happened near our neighborhood."

I remembered then that Rick lived near my grandparents.

"…and not long after the storm came through, I saw four fire trucks, two or three ambulances, and probably five police cars racing by our house. They stopped just down the road so I got out and ran down to see what was going on…it's not good, Pete."

"What is it, Rick?" Dad said, his voice trembling. Then realizing I was listening to every word, Dad gently nudged me into the cushioned bench against the wall and turned his back to me. He kept his voice low and quickly hung up, turning to race to the front of the bus.

"Dad…?" I said, following him.

When I finally made it to the front, he was leaning over our driver.

"Can't you go any faster, Dewayne?" Dad snapped.

"Peter, I'm doing the best I can," he said. "It's the best I can do without losing control of the bus. I'm not sure how long I will be able to maintain this speed. I don't know what we will run into ahead. You know the same line of storms is between us and home."

Dad shook his head and stepped back. "I'm sorry, Dewayne…just do the best you can, brother. I've got to get there as soon as possible to check on Emily and her parents."

"I know, Peter, I know. I'm just driving and praying," he said.

Just then Dewayne's phone rang. It was Sally.

In a quiet, almost guarded tone, Dewayne answered. "Hey honey, what's going on there?"

"It's bad, Dewayne. Most of the neighbors are outside talking about it. Information is beginning to spread around town bit by bit. Where are you?"

"Near the state line. We already turned around and are on our way back home. Do they know how much damage yet or—" his voice wavered—"if anyone's been hurt?"

"Well, everybody says that neighborhood near White Oaks was hit hardest. A couple of houses were leveled. Both at the end of Tipton Street."

My grandparents' street.

I felt empty inside, vacant.

Like some part of me had been blown away by the storm.

CHAPTER 3

Rain pounded the windshield of the bus just as Dewayne ended his call with Sally. He had to fight the wind just to keep the bus in its lane. The gusts caused the bus to rock; however, most of the wind was blowing from behind the bus, seemingly pushing us farther down the road. Dewayne knew exactly what that meant: a tailwind was propelling us right into the middle of the storm.

The rain started coming down even harder, in blinding sheets because of the wind. That, coupled with the darkness of the night, greatly reduced visibility for Dewayne. He turned the hazard flashers on and continued slowly, passing a few cars and trucks on the side of the road which had pulled over to the shoulder due to the storm.

It was hard driving for Dewayne, but he knew if there were any way possible to keep going, he couldn't stop. Dewayne had been driving buses for over twenty years, but later he said that was the hardest fifteen minutes he'd ever driven. Any other time, with weather like that, he too would have stopped on the shoulder to wait it out.

After a few minutes, the rain tapered off to a sprinkle and then stopped as fast as it had started. Just ahead, we could see the taillights of several cars stopped in our lane, along with the blue flashing lights of a Tennessee Highway Patrol car. Having driven for so many years on highways all over the country, Dewayne had seen his share of those lights stopping cars on the road. But his driving record was impeccable. Although he never had a speeding ticket, he was well aware of the owner of those lights. Something was different. It was odd to see several cars stopped by one patrol car. He thought there was no way they would be doing random checks in this kind of weather. He wondered what it could be.

He slowed the bus and took his place in line behind the cars already waiting. There was still a little wind, but Dewayne said he thought he'd be able to make up time on the road after he got past this unusual slow down.

The trooper ahead had other plans. He was diverting traffic toward an alternate route, one that couldn't be traveled as quickly as the interstate.

"What's the problem, officer?" asked Dewayne with a bit of agitation in his voice. "The road ahead looks perfectly clear."

"There's a tractor trailer overturned about ten miles down the road. Boxes are scattered everywhere. It looks like a barrier of wet cardboard. This detour is your only choice between here and there, my friend."

Dewayne took the exit and followed the detour route around the accident and got back on the Interstate as soon as possible. With the rain completely moved out of the area, it was a smooth but tense drive all the way into Inspiration.

Of course, Dad wanted Dewayne to drive straight to Grandma and Grandpa's house, but Dewayne knew he couldn't maneuver the bus around the narrow neighborhood streets. He explained to Dad that it would be best to take us to our house to get our truck, especially since our house was on the way there. Dad understood. Dewayne told Dad he would drive him over to Grandma's himself.

As we got closer to town, what we saw was eerie. There were only a few sections along the interstate with lights on. The rest were completely dark and we could hear sirens in the distance. We quickly exited and headed toward our house.

George called Kim, and she was there to meet us and said that they would take me to their house for the night. I always liked staying at George and Kim's house when Dad and Mom had date nights, but not tonight. Dad was relieved that I would be taken care of while he was trying to find out what was going on with Mom, Grandma and Grandpa. Dewayne parked the bus and drove Dad in his truck to Grandma and Grandpa's house.

The rest of the band stayed to take care of the equipment and get the bus refueled just in case we were able to get back on the road toward Richmond. They knew there would only be a short window of time if that were the case.

George and Kim took me home with them. Later I would hear how the rest of that early morning unfolded. When Dad and Dewayne made it to Tipton Street, they saw the destruction and devastation. At one end of the street were two Inspiration police cars blocking the road. Their lights were flashing and four officers were standing there talking. A small crowd of people stood nearby, just beyond the police cars.

Two ambulances were just leaving the scene. My dad knew someone was in the back of each ambulance, but the drivers didn't seem to be in too much of a hurry. Dad hoped it might be just a couple of people with minor injuries. He would soon learn the horrible truth: Grandma and Grandpa were about to be pronounced D.O.A. at the hospital.

At the far end of the street were three other police cars and two fire trucks with their lights flashing. They appeared to be parked in front of

Grandma and Grandpa's house. Dad grabbed Dewayne's arm and yelled "Come on!"

As they started to walk past the police cars, they were stopped by two of the officers standing there.

"You can't go down there."

In the dark, they didn't notice it was Dad.

Dad had become quite famous around town. There weren't too many people walking around with a #1 song on the charts. Dad had also been very active in raising money for various charities in the area.

About that time, one of the other officers turned around and noticed it was Dad.

"Peter. Thank God you're here," said Lieutenant Max who knew Dad well. "Let them go, guys. This is Peter Alford and Dewayne Davis."

Immediately, the officers backed off and let Dad and Dewayne pass through.

As Max walked down the road with them, he stopped and said, "Peter, I have to tell you something before you go down there. Two houses at the end of the street were hit hard. Emily's parents' house was one of them." Max paused, "They didn't make it, Peter."

"Didn't make it? What do you mean, Max?" Dad said as his voice trembled and tears began to well up in his eyes. "What about Emily? Where is she, Max? I have to see her."

"Was she there with them, Peter?" Max said with a puzzled look on his face.

"Yes. She was there. What do you mean 'Was she there?' Where is she?"

"We don't know, Peter. Her car was there, but we thought she was on tour with you on the bus and just left her car there. Where's Adam?"

"Adam's safe—with George and Kim. Where is Emily, Max?"

Without answering Dad, Max got on his radio and informed the officers and firemen down by the house that this is now a rescue effort.

"Guys, we're now looking for an adult female who was in the house at the time the storm hit."

Dad started to run down the road toward the house. Dewayne and Max were right behind him. They arrived at the house only to find remnants of what, at one time, had been a beautiful two-story house where Grandma and Grandpa lived. It was where we shared holiday meals and lazy Saturday afternoon barbeques on the back deck. But this was much different.

Dad stood there looking at thousands of splinters. The deck was gone, and clothes, broken furniture, and glass littered the ground. It looked like the house just exploded. There was a lawn chair, which once sat on the deck, hanging twisted from a tree overhead.

Mom's car seemed to be untouched. Hoping beyond hope, Dad rushed over to the car looking in the windows as if somehow Mom had been in the car when the storm hit.

"Emily!" Dad shouted. "Oh God, Emily, where are you?"

Dad dropped to his knees by the car with his hands covering his face.

Dewayne stood by him searching for something to say.

Suddenly the sound of music filled the air around them. It was the ringtone on Dad's phone. A few days earlier, he had set it up to ring that way when Mom called.

Dad was in such shock, he didn't even hear it ring.

"Peter!" Dewayne yelled, "Isn't that your phone?"

Dad looked up at Dewayne, not sure of what he was saying.

Again Dewayne said, "Peter, that's your phone. Isn't that the ringtone you set up for Emily's calls?"

Dad struggled to get his phone out of his pocket, only to realize he missed the call.

"Dewayne. It was Emily. She was calling me. She must be somewhere safe."

"Well, call her back, Peter."

Dad's phone rang again. "Emily, honey, where are you?"

Mom's voice was weak, and Dad could barely hear what she was saying.

"Peter…? I need…help."

"Where are you, Emily?"

"I think…leg is…broken."

"But where are you?" Dad shouted as if raising his voice would help locate her.

"I'm in a fi…" Then nothing.

"Emily! Where are you, baby?"

Nothing.

"Peter, where is she?" Dewayne said.

"I don't know."

Dad frantically dialed the phone, and it sounded like the call went through before going to voice mail.

Looking up at Dewayne, with a gasp, Dad said, "What should we do?"

Thinking quickly, Dewayne asked if Mom had the "Find My iPhone" app. She did, and Dad had her password in notes on his phone. Shaking so hard, Dad handed his phone to Dewayne who quickly found the password and entered it into the app.

"There she is, Peter," Dewayne said with growing excitement in his voice.

"She's out in the field, Dewayne."

As Dad ran into the field to find Mom, Dewayne gathered the first responders and told them they had found Emily's location on the phone. At once, an army of officers and volunteers descended on the field to find Mom. They frantically searched for what seemed to be an eternity to Dad. In reality, it took only minutes to get to where Mom was lying in the field.

Dewayne was the first to find her. It was easy to see that both of her legs appeared to be broken. Her left leg was lying at an angle like Dewayne had never seen a leg before. Her right leg was mangled. There were other noticeable minor cuts and scratches on her arms and legs, but what concerned Dewayne most was the fact that she was unconscious.

Dewayne called for Dad and the EMTs who joined the search in the field.

"Peter, I found her! She's over here!"

Dad and two EMTs were there in a flash. Dad knelt down beside Mom and started to pick her up. He was immediately stopped by the EMTs.

"Sir, you can't move her. She could have a broken back, or neck. Just stand back and we will take care of her."

The EMT was interrupted by Mom's trembling voice calling for dad.

"Peter? Are you here?"

"Yes honey, I'm here, and I'm not alone. There are people here who are going to help."

"Where are Mom and Dad? Have you seen them?"

As Dad was searching for words to answer, Mom asked, "Do you have Adam? Is he okay?"

"Yes, Adam is fine. He's with George and Kim."

Over the years, as I grew older, Dad has told me bits and pieces of the story. I believe it helps him to talk about it, and I really wanted to know what happened. He has always been wise in telling me what I wanted to know, while being sensitive to my age as we were talking. We've never made it past that point in the story because, at that point, Dad always choked up and I didn't want to push it.

A few weeks ago, though, Dewayne told me what he had witnessed out there in that field. Mom had tried to take a deep breath, and in a whisper she asked Dad to come closer to her. Dad leaned over as close as he could, and Mom said, "I love you so much Peter, tell Adam…"

Dewayne told me she finished her sentence but only Dad could hear what she said. She was so weak; she could barely make a sound. Dewayne always wondered what she said but had trouble finding the right time to ask Dad.

After she finished her sentence, Dewayne said she looked deeply into Dad's eyes. It was the last time they would see each other. She closed her eyes and was gone.

CHAPTER 4

After Mom's death, Dad drifted into a very dark place in his life. Other than caring for me, whom he loved deeply, he didn't seem to care about anything or anybody. He split off from the band and quit writing songs. Once I overheard him say, "The storm took everything but Adam away from me, and someday he will leave."

The label released two songs, which had not been released before Mom passed, and they did really well. Both songs quickly rose to the top of the charts. Dad believed it was because people felt sorry for him. His manager tried to convince him otherwise, but Dad wouldn't listen.

After dropping out of the band, Dad used the royalties from his songs to purchase another house. He said he couldn't live in the same house any longer because it only made him think about Mom.

Fortunately, one of his closest friends outside of the music business was Bob, a financial planner. Dad took Bob's advice and let him invest the rest of the money from the songs so we would have money to live on and my college education would be covered when the time came. Thank God for Bob. I'm not sure what would have happened to us had Dad not trusted him.

Although there was enough money to live on, no mortgage on the house, and my future college expenses would be covered, Dad began drinking and some of his spending habits made things a little tight at times.

As the years went by, Dad's drinking became worse and worse. By the time I was a senior in high school, against Bob's advice, Dad had been dipping into the investment account to the extent he couldn't pay the property taxes on the house. He got behind and eventually had to sell it. By that point, Dad was even dipping into my college fund. After selling the house, there was just enough money to pay off the back taxes, restore the funds in my college account, and buy a used doublewide trailer for us to have a place to live. He was also able to keep the truck.

Dad was forced to take on a couple of jobs just for us to get by. He was able to control his drinking enough to hold down a job driving a school bus in the mornings and afternoons. There were times, I've heard from other people, that some of the kids would say cruel things to Dad about once being a big star and now driving a bus. Somehow Dad kept his composure and also never told me. I know it had to cut him deeply. He loved people and loved music. But he just couldn't hold it together after losing Mom.

He was also a regular singing and playing in a ragtag band at Stick's, a local bar and grill, just down the road from where we lived. He played almost every Friday night outside of football season (Dad never missed one of my games) and every Saturday night. He lost his home, and lost his heart to write songs, but he never lost his ability to woo a crowd, even if he were just doing it for the money. Because I knew him so well,

I could tell he flipped a switch and went into performer mode. But after a show, he'd sink back into his depression again.

Although it was tough, I was making it through school. My grades were good; some would say "very good" as I was near the top of my class. I was vice president of the senior class. I was playing for our local high school team and was doing well—I had never given up my dream to be an NFL quarterback. Many days it was all that motivated me to keep going. I was acknowledged as an All-American, and according to several recruiting services including ESPN, I was the #1 quarterback recruit in the country. Every day there were several letters in the mail from college teams all over the country expressing their interest in me.

By my senior year, I had a girlfriend, Elizabeth, who's the most beautiful girl I have ever seen. With long brown hair and big green eyes, she has a smile that lights up any room she's in. She played in the marching band, worked at the Chick-fil-A off the interstate, and also loved working with the Special Olympics. Can you tell I'm a blessed guy?

It was her heart that first drew me to her. I first met her on a Wednesday night when George and Kim had taken me to a youth group meeting at their church. As Elizabeth shared her story that night, I sat silently and just listened as she spoke about the joy in her life. I desperately wanted that kind of joy, and found it that night.

I'll never forget leaving the church that night and asking Kim, "Who is *that* girl?"

"What girl?" Kim said with a smirk. She knew.

I just smiled and said, "You know…that girl."

"Oh, the one who shared her story tonight? Elizabeth?"

"Yeah, her. Elizabeth? Is that her name?"

"Yes, she's Bethany's daughter, plays clarinet in the band at school, and I believe her status was listed as 'Single' last time I checked Facebook." Kim smiled.

"Oh, I don't care about that. I was just wondering who she was. No big deal." Okay, so I wasn't a very good liar, and Kim picked up on it as fast as I said it.

Ignoring what I just said, Kim tried to sound casual: "Bethany and Elizabeth happen to be coming over for dinner tomorrow night. Do you want to join us?"

"Sure!" I said enthusiastically, too excited to hide my real feelings.

Elizabeth and her mom quickly became two of the people who have had an uncommon influence on my life. That meeting was the beginning of a very special relationship, which is stronger than ever today. The rest of that year we did everything together. Whether it was school, church, marching band competitions, or football games, we were together.

+ + +

By the time my senior football season ended, I held almost every high school quarterback record in the state. Elizabeth and the band won the state marching band championship for the second year in a row. Life seemed to be going better.

But I have to say, the football recruiting scene was kind of weird for me. The only person I really wanted attention from was Elizabeth. But there were college coaches at our school wanting to meet with me every week. My cell phone was ringing all the time.

National Signing Day was coming up in a few months and I had a very important decision to make. I had to decide where I was going to play college football. National Signing Day is the first day high school players sign a National Letter of Intent to attend and play for a specific college team. It's an agreement between the player and the school. The player agrees to play football and attend the school full time. The school agrees to provide an athletic scholarship to the athlete. If the student does not attend that school, and wants to go to another school, there is a penalty. The player will have to attend the next school full-time for one year without playing. The athlete will also lose one season of eligibility to play college sports. So signing that letter is a pretty serious commitment for any student athlete.

The good part of the deal is that after a player signs a National Letter of Intent with one school, all other schools stop recruiting that player. Although my mind wasn't made up at the time, I was ready for the process to be over.

As with most high school athletes fortunate enough to be recruited to play college sports, my decision really only came down to a few primary schools. Ole Miss was at the top of the list. It's where a Coach by the name of Hugh Freeze and his coaching staff had impressed me. I had also met his wife, Jill, and she reminded me of my mom. The other schools were the University of Utah because of their coaching staff, USC because of its great tradition, and the University of Tennessee at Chattanooga, which was only twenty minutes from my house.

I added a small Christian school, Lee University, to the list because they were also close to home and had just added a football program. My dad's alma mater, Lee, had always been a place I loved to go for summer camps, basketball games, baseball games, and concerts. Several of my friends from high school planned to go to Lee.

Of course, no one thought I would sign with Lee on National Signing Day. The good money was on Ole Miss for a lot of reasons. I always wanted to play in the SEC (I had scholarship offers from almost every school in the conference), and it was no secret how much I liked the coaching staff there. I was pretty sure Ole Miss was where I wanted to play.

+ + +

The only thing that could hold me back was the fact that Dad would be in Inspiration and I would be in Oxford, Mississippi, about a five and a half hour drive away. Dad reassured me several times that he would be at every game and he was totally comfortable with me going to school there.

No matter how many times he told me, I always wondered how my dad really felt about me going to school that far away from home. I couldn't stand the thought of going if he really wanted me to stay closer to home. Dad's life seemed to be centered on me. I was the reason he still played music at Stick's. I was the reason he drove a school bus. I was also the reason he even talked about fighting the temptation to drink. He centered his life around me because I was all he had. I didn't want my leaving the area to be the reason he gave up.

Depending on the distance of the school, almost every one of them addressed this situation with me. Many of the schools farther away would try to tell me it would be good for Dad to begin to focus on himself if I were away at school, while most of the schools closer to home would play the "you should be near your dad" card. One alumni, from a school which wasn't even on my short list, offered to get my dad a house rent free near their school if I would sign with them, which is clearly against NCAA rules.

There were also a lot of good schools, like the ones on my short list and a few others, who I believed were shooting straight with me. Although I had not named a leader, I guess the reason all the recruiting services made mention that Ole Miss had the best shot at my signature was because I would mention them, and how much I liked the coaching staff in every interview. That wasn't intentional on my part. It just felt right there and it wasn't as far from home as some of the others at the top of my list.

All the attention really started to get to me. It got old fast. I love to play and I love to lead, so being a quarterback felt like a calling in life for me. I just didn't enjoy all the interviews and spotlight on my every move. There were even people talking about the color of shirts I would wear and how those colors were associated with different schools.

My focus was on getting better every day.

Hearing the positive things people said about me as a quarterback didn't make me gloat; it made me assess my game and want to be better. I remember Barry, one of my dad's best friends, say, "Don't let the accolades make you boast, or the harsh words discourage you. Neither the accolades, nor the harsh words, define your self-worth."

It always made me feel good when Dad would read a quote someone said about the way I played. One day he was reading a quote from one of the major recruiting services, either Rivals or Scout, which said:

"Alford is a solid quarterback who plays with great poise and form... he is a marvel for people to watch on film from the standpoint of fundamentals... yet when he's on the field and the game is on the line, he can be a gunslinger... when the heat is on, he can play with reckless abandon, improvise, and keep a play alive reminiscent of future Hall of Famer, Ben Roethlisberger. He isn't afraid of a challenge, and deserves the nickname Captain Clutch. The game never gets too big for him. Adam's overall grade is similar to that of Blake Bortles when he was coming out of college. Blake is one of the hottest young quarterbacks in the NFL."

Dad continued to read: *"He is a great leader on and off the field with a charismatic and magnetic personality, one..."*

I remember feeling embarrassment and excitement at the same time. The embarrassment just came from hearing all that stuff about me. The excitement came from an idea I had as dad finished reading the quote.

"...who never meets a stranger."

"Hey dad."

"What, son?" Dad said as he was looking up from the article.

"There is someone I want you to meet, someone I don't want to be a stranger to you."

"Who is that?"

"Dad, I want you to visit Ole Miss with me and meet the coaches there."

"Okay, when do you want to go?"

"Wait—did you just say you would go with me?"

"Of course, Adam. What red-blooded American male would not want to visit that beautiful campus in Oxford, Mississippi?" Then he winked at me.

That was the first time I had heard Dad even hint at the fact that he knew there were any other girls in the world since we lost Mom.

+ + +

I knew he was kidding with me about girls, but he did say he would go.

Without wasting a second, I immediately called Coach Freeze.

"Hey, Coach,"

"What's up, Adam?" He had given me his cell number in case I ever had any questions, and he had my name and number saved in his contacts.

"Is it okay for me to come for an official visit this week with my dad?"

"Of course it is, Adam. You are always welcome here. This week would be a great time to take your official visit. You know we are playing LSU here in Oxford on Saturday."

"Coach, I always know who the Rebels are playing. I'll see you this weekend."

"Sounds great. We will see you then. I'll have someone contact you to set it up."

"Great. Thanks, Coach." As I recall, I was so excited I disconnected the call without saying bye.

My team had a bye in the playoffs that Friday night, so dad and I loaded up the old F-150 early Friday morning and headed to Oxford.

"Dad, you've had this old truck since I was ten. When are you going to get a new one so I can have this one?"

"Adam, you know I can't buy a new truck right now. But when I do, this one will be all yours, buddy."

It was a beautiful day and the drive to Oxford was a great experience for us. It had been a long time since I had seen dad stay sober for more than a week. Weekends, while singing at Stick's, were usually the worst. But this weekend, Dad was all sober, and all mine.

I remember thinking, maybe I can get him to move to Oxford and it would be like this all the time.

Upon arrival in Oxford, my heart was pounding. At one point, Dad even asked, in a kidding way, if I was having a heart attack.

"Dad, do you realize where we are? I could actually be playing here someday. I think they like me."

"Adam, not 'someday', you could be here next year. Of course they like you. What's not to like about you, buddy?" Dad seemed happy he was able to get me to crack a smile.

We both laughed.

"I love you, Dad."

"I love you too, Adam. I wish your mom could see you now"

"Me, too. Maybe she can."

"Maybe she can, buddy. You know the Bible talks about there being a great cloud of witnesses."

I remember being surprised that Dad mentioned something in the Bible. He hadn't mentioned God or the Bible since Mom died. I actually thought he was blaming God, but don't remember him ever mentioning that he did. It was just a feeling. Either way, it made me feel good just thinking Mom may be watching from Heaven.

As we drove onto campus, Dad said, "Hey look, Adam, the speed limit on campus is '18 MPH'. Do you know why?"

"Yep. Because that was Archie Manning's number when he played here."

"Archie who?" Dad said in another attempt to make me laugh.

Of course we both knew 'Archie who?' is how some misguided fans of an opposing team were taunting Archie and his gang of Rebels prior to the Rebels running them out of the stadium to the tune of a 38-0 victory.

Dad did get a smile out of me on that one.

I remember being so happy during that trip. Dad actually seemed to have fun for the first time since the night of that terrible storm.

CHAPTER 5

I was treated like royalty on campus. We were greeted by people around town who weren't even part of the team or athletic department. They knew me by name and told me how much they wanted to see me play in Oxford. For some reason that wasn't weird like all the interviews and media attention. It just felt like home. The whole town was beginning to feel like family.

I was able to sit in on a meeting with the current quarterbacks, and was also able to meet with most of the coaching staff. They told me how I could fit into the program and how they planned to develop their offensive game plans around me. Even the coaches on the defensive side of the ball greeted me and let me know how much they wanted me to be part of the team.

While all that was going on, Dad was getting the more academic view of the school. He was impressed by the number of Academic All-Americans and Rhodes Scholars associated with the school. At some point during that day, he met the Director of Bands for Ole Miss, and was happy to learn they had played one of his songs during their halftime show a few years back.

Everything came together in such a way during our visit that Dad and I decided it was time to make a public commitment to the school. That would give me the opportunity to openly start recruiting other players I had become friends with at various football camps to join me at Ole Miss. I also hoped the media storm would die down after I finally committed.

I verbally committed on the spot with the coaches and we decided to make it public at that time. Because I was the highest rated quarterback coming out of high school that year, the news of my verbal commitment to Ole Miss was discussed on every major sports show in America. Although it wasn't a big surprise, it seemed to be newsworthy.

The media storm got worse for a while. There were several requests for interviews, and I did a few. Then it died down some. I'm told that's how the 24- hour news cycle works.

However, back in our hometown, the news cycle lasted a little bit longer.

The owner of the club where my dad had been playing on the weekends wasn't happy to hear the news. Although he didn't care about football and couldn't care less where I would be playing, he was concerned how that might impact where his main draw talent (my dad) would be playing. He was afraid he might lose him.

He pondered what he would do if Dad decided to move to Oxford to be close enough to attend every home game without having to drive five and a half hours to get there. He couldn't come up with another performer who would bring in as much cash on the weekends as Dad. He knew that if Dad left, it would be devastating to his business. No Peter Alford would mean no Saturday night crowd at Stick's.

+ + +

After we returned home from our visit to Oxford, Dad and I were surrounded with a strange mixture of well-wishers, and a few fans from other teams digging at us (it seemed to be all in fun) because I didn't verbally commit to their team. I wasn't sure about all of them, but I believe they were mostly just kidding.

What we didn't know was that Roger, the owner of Stick's, had something else in mind. While his scheme was all planned out, he took his time before showing his hand.

From time to time he would hit dad with vague contract language written in a half-baked contract they had signed for Dad to sing at Stick's on Saturday nights. He even took backhanded swipes at threatening to sue Dad for breach of contract if he decided to move away during that time. There were fourteen months left on the contract.

Although I didn't know about any of that at the time, Dad never let it shake him. He knew Roger didn't have a leg to stand on when it came to forcing him to stay in the area just to sing on weekends. He never let me know anything about what Roger said because he was concerned it might impact my final decision on signing day. Besides, what Roger had to say didn't matter anyway.

Dad kept performing on weekends because we needed the money.

Then one day, the week before National Signing Day, I walked into the club one Saturday afternoon to see if Dad needed any help setting up for the night.

"Hi Roger, where's my dad?"

"Uh, he already has everything set up for tonight and stepped out for a minute. He should be back in a bit. How are you doing, Adam?"

I had no idea about the plot that was about to unfold.

"I'm fine, pretty excited about signing day coming up this week."

"I bet you are." Roger said with some excitement in his voice. "I know your dad is real proud of you, Adam."

This was the first real conversation Roger and I ever had. He was usually pretty distant and never asked me about football, school, or anything.

"He seems pretty excited, Roger. Maybe things will work out and he can move to Oxford so he can be at all the home games. That would be great."

"Yeah, I've heard him talk about that some."

"What has he told you, Roger? Do you think he would really do that?"

"Well, I know he has talked about it. At least he told me he has thought about it. But…"

"But what?"

"It's just that, aww… never mind. It doesn't really matter."

"What doesn't really matter, Roger?"

"Seriously, Adam. It's best that you not know."

Thinking back, I know he was baiting me, and I fell right into it.

"Best that I not know what? Roger, you can't do me like that. If there is something I need to know, you've just got to tell me. What is it?"

"Alright, but you can't mention a word of it to your dad or he will kill me."

"I promise; I won't tell a soul. What is it?"

Roger began to play out his well-planned scheme.

"It's just that I overheard him talking to someone the other day about how he really wanted you to stay here and play close to home. He said something about his finances being too tight to move right now, and didn't know what he would do when you actually moved off to Oxford."

"What are you saying, Roger?"

"Well, Adam," Roger continued "the truth is that he doesn't have the money to move, and he can't bring himself to tell you how much he really wants you to stay at home and play here. I can tell he gets more anxious as signing day is just around the corner."

"Really? He said that to you?"

By that time, the hook was set and he was reeling me in.

"Yes. I'm sorry to be the one to tell you, Adam, but it's really killing him. He would never let you know because he cares so much about you and wants you to be happy no matter what it does to him."

"Then why…"

"Adam," Roger interrupted me "I'm sure he would like to move. It's just that the money isn't there right now and he doesn't want to be looked at by the media as being a selfish dad. I'm sure if they knew how much he wants you to stay here, they would crucify him on every sports show in America. That's why no one can know but you. I guess you could pull a surprise on signing day and let on like it's a total change of heart or something.

"Surprise?"

"Yeah, like maybe you changed your mind for some sentimental reason like wanting to stay close to where your mom is buried or something like that. Anything but putting it off on your dad."

"What am I going to do, Roger? I really thought he might…"

"Your dad really wants you to be happy, Adam. He loves you more than you know. He just doesn't want you to know that he can't move right now, and that he won't be able to come to many of your games."

My signing decision didn't seem so clear anymore.

+ + +

While Roger went to stock the bar, I thought through what he had said. A couple minutes later, Dad walked in the front door and seemed surprised to see me there.

"Hey, guys. What's up?" Dad said.

"Oh, Adam and I were just shooting the breeze about National Signing Day coming up, Peter. I know you must be so proud of your boy." Roger nodded my way and smiled as he continued wiping down the bar.

"I sure am. I wish his mom could see him now."

"I know you do, Peter. I know you do."

Roger glanced at me with an "I told you so" look and headed back to the stockroom.

Before Dad could ask what was going on, I said, "Well, I guess you are all set up here for tonight, Dad. I just came by to see if you needed any help."

"I'm all good here, Adam. Thanks for the offer though." With intended sarcasm he added, "I'm really going to miss this old place when we move to Oxford." Then he winked at me. I wasn't sure if he was kidding or not.

I tried to smile but knew I had to get out of there. I would have been so excited if I hadn't just had that conversation with Roger. Everything suddenly seemed upside down.

I could do what was best for Dad.

Or I could do what was best for me.

But not both.

+ + +

The next few days were tough. Those sleepless nights I would lie in bed, thinking through the possibilities of what might happen with the various choices before me. I knew the most exciting day of my life was approaching fast, but I still didn't know what to do about it. This was becoming one of the hardest decisions of my life.

Dad could see that I seemed to be somewhat anxious. A couple of times he asked me how I was doing, and I did my best to reassure him.

"It's all good, Dad. I'm just ready for it to be over."

What Roger had said that day sank deep into my heart. I loved Ole Miss, and I loved the thought of playing there. But I loved my dad more than any of that, and there was no way I wanted to leave Dad by himself.

Maybe my choice was pretty easy after all.

On the night before Signing Day, I drove my car to the parking lot of Lee University's new football stadium. It was nice, but very small. It certainly wasn't the caliber of a Division I stadium. It would only seat 8,000 fans.

I made my way onto the field through a gate that had been left unlocked. There were a few security lights on that allowed me to find my way around the stands.

I remember climbing up the stands at the 50-yard line. I stared at the field with a heavy heart. Lee is an awesome school, and if I weren't able to play college football at the highest level, I would have loved to stay and play for Lee.

The next five minutes would be the toughest for me since I heard the news about Mom's death.

I sat in the stands. With tears in my eyes and my hands a bit shaky, I called Coach Freeze knowing the trajectory of my life was about to change.

Of course he knew it was me calling. I'm sure he wondered why I would be calling the night before I was about to sign.

"Adam, how are you man? Are you excited about tomorrow?"

"Um, Coach, I need to tell you something."

"What's wrong, Adam? You don't sound like yourself."

"Coach, I can't do it."

"Can't do what, Adam?"

"I can't come. I can't sign with Ole Miss tomorrow."

Ole Miss passed on other strong quarterbacks who had interest in coming. The plan was to only sign one quarterback that year, and I was their guy.

They were set to have the #1 recruiting class in the country, and as the headliner for that class, I was about to flip to little known Lee University. The ramifications could be huge for the Rebels. I had been very active in getting other standout players around the country to take visits to Ole Miss. I was concerned they would be upset with me, although I knew they instantly fell in love with the school and coaching staff after they visited. We had big plans to win championships together.

The pause by Coach Freeze after I said I couldn't come wasn't long, but to me it seemed like forever.

"I don't understand, Adam. What happened?"

"Coach, it's my dad. I just can't leave him here alone. I am going to have to stay here and play for Lee University."

"Wasn't he thinking about moving to Oxford with you?"

"That's what he told me, Coach, but I wasn't sure he was serious. Later I found out from a friend of his that he is just telling me that so I won't change my mind. He knows how much I want to come to Ole Miss."

"Does he know you have changed your mind?"

"No, sir. And I'm not going to tell him. I gave my word that I wouldn't let Dad know what I was told."

"Do you trust the person who told you?"

"I don't know. But I can't take that chance. I just don't want to hurt him. First, my mom dying in the tornado, and now I would be leaving when he can't leave. I just can't do that, Coach."

"I can only imagine how you must feel, Adam. You know how much we want you here. I know you want to be here and help us win championships. There is no doubt how important we believe you are to this program. I also believe you know how we feel about family. You do what you believe is best for you and your family. Everything else will work out. I know Coach Jabes there at Lee, and he's a great guy."

Tears began to fill the corners of my eyes. "I knew you would say that, and that makes this even harder."

"Adam, as a dad myself, I believe you should discuss this with your father before you make your final decision. It seems only fair for him to know. Either way, I'm praying for you to make the best decision, and I'll be here for you if you need to talk."

"Thanks, Coach. Go Rebs!"

"Take care, Adam."

I disconnected the call with a heavier heart than I had when I dialed his number. I knew that once I signed the National Letter of Intent, there would be no turning back.

+ + +

On the morning of National Signing Day, the high school had made arrangements for me to sign my Letter of Intent in the gym in front of the student body. Several people in the community, and a rather large contingent of media who had gathered to cover what many considered to be the "main event" of the sports world that day, were present.

As Dad and I were getting ready to go to the ceremony at the school, I knew I would have to tell him about my decision. There was a part of me that wanted him to be surprised that I was going to stay close to home and play at Lee, while the wiser part of me knew Coach Freeze was right and I had to tell him.

I basically took the middle road, and told him at the last minute. I just didn't want him to feel betrayed, or that I had left him out of knowing before everyone else knew. Somehow I think he knew something was up by the way his voice sounded when he asked me a question before we left home for the school.

"Are you excited, buddy?" That was my open door to tell him.

"I am, Dad, but I need to tell you something before we go."

"What's that?"

"Well…" I paused. "I've changed my mind."

"Changed your mind? About what?"

"About going to Ole Miss."

"What? It's perfect for you, Adam. What do you mean, you've changed your mind about going to Ole Miss?"

For a second, I wanted to call back and ask if they still had a scholarship for me and do what I really wanted to do. There was something in dad's tone that made me think he really wanted me to go there. Then I remembered what Roger told me and convinced myself dad was just playing along so I wouldn't know how he really felt about me leaving.

"Well, Dad…"

"I know you're kidding," Dad interrupted. "Right?"

"No Dad, I'm not kidding. I called and told them last night."

"Adam, what are you talking about?"

"Dad, I've decided to stay here and play for Lee."

"Adam, Lee is a great school, everybody knows that. But it's certainly not big time college football. Why would you want to stay here?"

I knew there was no explanation I could give that he'd believe, but I had to try the one possibility that might work. "It's Mom, dad. It's because of Mom."

"Your mom?"

"Dad, I can't explain it. This is home. Mom is buried not too far from here. I know she can't come to my games, but I can play close to where she is buried."

When I said that, I knew how silly it sounded, but that's all I could say at the time. I couldn't make up anything better. Roger had scripted out what I was saying.

"Buddy, you know I will support you all the way, no matter what decision you make. But I can't imagine you turning down a full ride to play in the SEC."

Beginning to get choked up, I lied again and said, "I just don't want to leave this area at this point in my life."

Tears began streaming down my face.

Dad grabbed me and wrapped me in a big bear hug. He thought I was crying about the emotion of not wanting to leave. The real reason was that I really wanted to go to Ole Miss.

Nonetheless, Dad's words were encouraging: "Adam, a few years ago, when we all started to notice there was something special about you as a quarterback, I knew the day would come when you would have the opportunity to play for some big college."

I nodded and wondered where he was going with this.

He continued, "Honestly, at the time, I dreaded it. I couldn't stand the thought of you going away. But the trip to Oxford changed everything. I knew you would fit perfectly, and flourish there. So after that trip, not only was I okay with you going there, I was actually excited about it. After seeing the town and the school, meeting the coaching staff, and all the people around town, I wanted to move there, too. Are you totally sure about this, son?"

Again, I wanted to tell dad the truth, call Ole Miss and, if still possible, sign with them. But then I remembered Roger's words about Dad wanting to move but not being able to because of finances. I convinced myself to stick to my story and do what I felt was best for dad.

"Yes, Dad, I'm sure. This is exactly what I want to do."

I was trying to convince myself this was what I wanted to do because I really wanted to make Dad happy.

"What did Coach Freeze say?"

"Same as you. He wants me to come, but he understood. That's just the kind of guy he is, Dad."

"Well then, Adam, as hard as it is for me to believe this is what you really want to do, there is no way I would stand in your way. Just know I will be there with you today, and I will stand behind whatever you decide."

"I know, Dad. Thanks. That means the world to me."

CHAPTER 6

When we arrived on campus, the high school parking lot was already full. Students were having to park in overflow parking areas because of the TV news trucks and people from the community who were there for the announcement. There were standing room only spots available in the gym where I was about to sign my National Letter of Intent.

There was a special buzz in the air that morning. It would be the first time anyone from our high school had the opportunity to sign a scholarship to play football at a Division I school. D1 is the highest level of college football, and I was fortunate enough to have a choice to play at that level.

It didn't seem to matter to most of them that I was going to sign with an out of state school. Our community is close. All week I had heard from people in the community telling me how proud they were of me. When I walked in the gym, there were several people who were wearing Ole Miss apparel in support of me. Of course, that made what I was about to do even harder.

Although I had offers from schools from coast to coast, I verbally and publically committed to Ole Miss and had stuck with that commitment throughout the process after I announced it. There were only two school hats out on the table in front of the chair where I would be sitting: Ole Miss and Lee University. If there were any doubts where I would sign before that day, the doubts were, let's say, off the table.

Traditionally, when there is some ambiguity about who a player may sign with, there are three to four hats representing his top choices out on the table. When it's time for the announcement and the official signing, the player picks up the hat for the team of his choice and puts it on announcing to the world where he will go to school.

My signing was going to be the first of the day covered by ESPN. The storyline was well known. My dad had been a famous singer-songwriter, my family went through a widely reported tragedy, and I was rated as the #1 quarterback recruit in the country. Like the rest of the recruiting season, there were times when it kind of felt good, and times when I just wanted to duck and hide.

I know it was a little strange having only two hats sitting on the table even though there was no doubt, at least in the public's eyes where I was going to school. Still, we had to find a way to make the announcement. The truth is, I just didn't know what to do. I was confused. I was making a decision based on a lie. I just didn't know it.

Because of my commitment, and the three other players making their announcements which would follow me that morning, everybody believed this day would garner the highest rating ever for National Signing Day for ESPN. Nobody, including me, knew what was about to unfold because of my surprise announcement.

There was an uneventful start to the show. Everything seemed scripted and fell in place perfectly until the TV lights were turned on and I was sitting at the table with my dad and high school coach beside me.

Later, I learned that ESPN Analyst, Jordan Cassidy, was the only one to notice something just wasn't right. Although he couldn't put his finger on it, he knew something was not right. He had been an investigative reporter for 18 years prior to joining ESPN. He was an expert in body language to the extent that one might say he could read people like a book. Although he didn't know why, or exactly what would happen, somehow he had an inclination that I was not going to be signing my National Letter of Intent with Ole Miss that day.

Somehow he sensed that he was about to be part of a breaking story that would rock the college football world, but couldn't share it because he wasn't sure what to share. Sometimes you can know something is going to happen, and yet have to let the script play out on its own. After all, he was there to report the news, not make it.

He just didn't know if I were about to pull a surprise hat from under the table or delay signing that day. That wouldn't be unheard of, but my commitment had been airtight since the day I committed.

Jordan had five minutes until airtime and only a couple of ways he could confirm his suspicion. He could look behind the table while he was acting like he was checking the ESPN mic, or try to get someone at Ole Miss on the phone and ask straight up. Option 2 was out of the question. There would be no way for a reporter to get a Division I college football coach on the phone for an unplanned call at that moment, and if he did, he knew no one on the coaching staff would take anything away from my opportunity to share my decision publically.

Later, Jordan told me he called his ESPN counterparts who were in Oxford for National Signing Day, to report on my signing and the others who would be signing their National Letter of Intent to play for Ole Miss. With only five minutes to work, he knew he was under a crunch for time. The problem was that no one was answering his call.

What he didn't know was that the Ole Miss coaching staff was already working on what they would do as a result of me not signing with them. The ESPN people there knew something big was happening and were trying to get the scoop on whatever was going on.

Jordan decided to let the story play out.

Finally, the wait was over and he was about to go on air in… 5-4-3-2-1: "You're on," said one of the producers.

"Ladies and Gentlemen, I am Jordan Cassidy, and we are here at Inspiration High School in Inspiration, Tennessee, to kick off our National Signing Day show with the #1 rated high school quarterback in the country, everybody's All-American quarterback, Adam Alford. We are about to see which hat…" He paused because 5 minutes ago, this was just part of the script, but now he doubted what was about to happen. He began again, "…which hat Adam Alford will select, and where he will invest the next several years of his life playing the game he loves."

The cameras panned over to the table where we were seated.

Under his breath, and leaning away from the mic, my dad asked one more time, "Are you absolutely sure this is what you want to do?"

"Yeah, Dad, I'm alright," I choked out.

Dad was very concerned about my tone and the words I gave as an answer, but at that point there was nothing else left for him to do. As a performer, he knew the show must go on. He told me he would be by my side and that he would support my choice. And that's what he was doing.

The red light on the camera in front of me was my cue to begin. I adjusted the mic and paused. I had re-written my speech over and over a dozen times. I had it printed out and in front of me, but the words were still hard to read because the most important part of what I was about to say wasn't from my heart.

"Ladies and gentlemen, friends, school administrators, coaches and teachers, I want to begin by saying thank you. Thank you for being there for me through the highs and lows, through wins, and losses. To my teammates over the past four years, thank you for your hard work on and off the field. We accomplished a lot together. I wish my mom were here today. That's the one thing I want more than anything else."

I paused to wipe a tear. "But I am happy to be sitting here next to my best friend in the world, my dad." I glanced over at him. "We've been through a lot together haven't we?" I wiped another tear from my eye. "This decision has been much harder than you may think. It's an important decision that will impact the rest of my life. I have decided to play college football…" I paused again and this time stared right at the Ole Miss hat, which I really wanted to pick up, and said… "right here near home at Lee University." I picked up the Ole Miss hat and put it on.

The crowd was stunned and confused.

I said one thing but did something totally different. I said Lee, but put on the Ole Miss hat.

Dad leaned over to me and whispered,

"Did you mean to pick up the Ole Miss hat?"

I didn't know what to say. It was that awkward moment no one wants to live through. I didn't know what to do. So I just took the Ole Miss hat off, laid it back down on the table, picked up the Lee hat and put it on.

Jordan handled it like a pro on air. He didn't mention the fact that he knew something was about to happen, but he also he never thought it would be Lee where I would play football.

Jordan continued, "Well folks, that's why we show up on National Signing Day. We wonder what the coaches at Ole Miss are thinking right now. Next we will take you to Wichita, Kansas, for the second signing of the day, Jeremiah Clark, who is the #2 Quarterback in the country. He is the one many thought would overtake Adam as the #1 quarterback recruit because of the amazing second half of his senior year. He holds many of the quarterback passing and rushing career records in his state, and that's with only playing half of his senior year after he broke his non-throwing arm in a pick-up basketball game back in August. We'll be back with Jeremiah Clark's decision after this short break."

Then he cut away to a commercial.

+ + +

Unlike me, I knew Jeremiah was planning on having a lot of hats on the table. He had been uncommitted and quiet throughout the recruiting process as he was holding scholarship offers from as many schools as I was. At one of the All-Star games he told me the only school out of the running for his signature was Ole Miss, because I already committed to them. I was told his parents didn't even know where he was going. There were rumors he made a private commitment somewhere, but the school's name would change with whichever recruiting site you wanted to believe.

The TV lights were turned off in Inspiration and the crew started to pack their bags. Lights were flipped on in Wichita awaiting the network to come back from a commercial break.

No one knew that Jeremiah had called Ole Miss right after I made my announcement, and asked if they had a scholarship available for him. He immediately made a private commitment to them. That all basically happened within the time of a commercial break. Obviously, the coaches there were ecstatic.

After the commercial it was Jeremiah's time to be in the spotlight. With five other hats from major football programs around the country on the table, Jeremiah Clark surprised the world by pulling a red Ole Miss hat out from below the table and placed it on his head proclaiming he was going to sign with Ole Miss. He had an Ole Miss hat in his truck. During the commercial break he asked his dad to go out and get it for him. His dad knew exactly what he was going to do when he saw my surprise announcement. ESPN, which was already set for the split screen at Ole Miss for my announcement, quickly flipped the switch to cover the Ole Miss coaches' reactions.

News of Jeremiah's decision to play for Ole Miss quickly spread and everyone around me was talking about it within seconds of it being aired. He was about to get to do what I really wanted to do. I was happy that the coaching staff at Ole Miss would not suffer because of my decision.

Later, Jeremiah told me the reason he never committed anywhere was that he really wanted to go to Ole Miss. He said that he was on the verge of committing the day I committed, but didn't pull the trigger fast enough to beat me. Once I committed, his decision was all about who his second choice would be. It was actually a good day for everyone except me.

+ + +

Dad and I went in a back room to sign the papers and have them faxed to Lee University. We told the coach at Lee that morning, so they had the papers ready for us. I signed first, then it was Dad's turn.

He paused, looked at me, and said, "You know it's not binding if I don't sign don't you?"

This was my last chance. I hesitated, then realized Jeremiah had already announced and was about to sign. He had respected my initial commitment and was searching for his second choice. After I backed out and he committed, there was no way I could change my mind. That's when it really hit me. It was over. I wasn't going to go to Ole Miss.

I looked up at dad and said, "Just sign the darn paper," and walked away from the table.

Dad signed and walked over to me and said, "Let's go."

He wanted us to get out of the gym and home before any leftover media people could interview me. We faxed the Letter of Intent we signed and slipped out the back of the gym and made our way to Dad's truck before anyone could stop us for questions. Just as we were getting to the truck, we noticed Jordan was standing there waiting for us. He pleaded with Dad to allow him to ask me one question, totally off the record.

Dad said, "Off the record?"

"Completely off the record," Jordan replied.

"Okay, but just one question then we have to go."

"Adam," Jordan asked me "why did you pick up that hat?"

"Sir?" was my only reply.

"Just before you announced your decision to go to Lee, you seemed to wipe a tear, then you said this decision was harder than we might think. When you said that, you were staring right at the Ole Miss hat. Then you said, 'Right near here at Lee University'. But you didn't pick up the Lee hat. Why not? Why did you pick up the Ole Miss hat and put it on?"

At that moment, Dad saw the expression on my face, and knew something was up. Although he knows me better than anyone else in the world, he had missed all the clues and unintentional hints I had been giving. He had asked me several times if I was sure, but he missed what was below the surface.

He looked at me and said, "My God son, what have you done? What have we done? I should have known. Why?"

I couldn't hold back any longer. "Dad, I love you more than you could ever imagine. I just couldn't put you in the position of being torn between wanting to be with me and not being able to move because of money and losing your job working for Roger."

"Losing my job with Roger? I told him when you first committed to Ole Miss that I was moving and that I was excited about going to Oxford. There are a ton of places to play music there which pay well over what little Roger is paying me. I told him I had already spoken with several friends who have played Oxford, and they told me it's one of the best places in the world for somebody like me. I told Roger that more than once. I just didn't want to tell you for sure because I didn't want anyone to think I had influenced you to sign with Ole Miss just so I could have cool places to play music while making a boat load more money."

As Dad told me that, I could feel the blood drain from my face. He said it was one of the only times he had seen me speechless.

Jordan interjected, "Guys, it's probably best for me to leave now. I gave you my word I would only ask one question and keep it off the record, and I intend to keep my word. The less I know right now, probably the better. All I ask is that, if you do give an interview later, to let it be with me."

"You got it. Thanks," Dad replied without ever looking up at Jordan.

He looked at me and said, "Why didn't you pick up that hat, Adam?"

I didn't say a word.

Again, Dad said, "Adam, why didn't you pick up the Lee hat?"

"Because I really wanted to go to Ole Miss," I said in a trembling voice.

"Then why didn't you say that, son? Why did you tell me you wanted to go to Lee when you really wanted to go to Ole Miss?"

"Roger." was my only reply.

"Roger? What do you mean Roger? Is it because of something Roger said to you, Adam?"

"Yes sir." I couldn't bear to look at him.

"What did he say, Adam?"

"He said it was killing you that I was moving away, and that you wouldn't tell me because you didn't want to be selfish influencing my decision. He made me promise not to tell anyone he told me that, and that I could just tell people that I wanted to stay close by and play near where Mom is buried."

"Roger used me, and brought your mom and where she is buried into this?"

"I'm sorry…really sorry, Dad."

"That lying, no good—!" Dad slammed his fist into the side of the truck and made a dent it would take a body shop to pull out.

"Get in the truck, Adam!" Dad shouted.

"I didn't know what to do. Are you mad at me?"

There was an extended delay before he replied, "No, son, I'm not mad at you. I'm just torn between letting you watch me kill that lying snake and making you stay outside while I do it."

"Dad, you can't—it will be okay. Just don't do anything stupid."

But I could tell he wasn't listening.

+ + +

Before I knew it, we arrived in the parking lot at Stick's. Dad jumped out of the truck and rushed inside. He left the truck door open, and I could hear the ruckus beginning to erupt inside. I got out of the truck and started to go inside when I noticed a patrol car pull into the parking lot. It was Sheriff Chris Birmingham. Chris, and his brother Keith, who is an EMT, had been friends with my dad since they were in elementary school.

Chris and Keith had followed Dad and me after he saw Dad slam his fist into the truck at the high school parking lot. They were at the signing ceremony and knew something was wrong. They had never seen Dad in a rage like that before.

"What's wrong with your dad?" Chris asked me as he passed by without breaking stride on his way inside.

"I think he is going to kill Roger."

Chris entered Stick's to find Roger on the floor being pounded by Dad. There was no sign of him letting up. I heard Dad use words I had never heard him use before.

Chris grabbed my dad under his arms and pulled him off Roger, pretty much throwing him across the room. After making a quick assessment of Roger's condition, Keith started to help Roger, who looked pretty bloody. Later, we discovered it was just a bloody nose.

Chris helped Dad sit up on the floor and lean against a wall. He had his face in his hands and was weeping profusely as Chris was trying to calm him down.

"What in the heck were you thinking, Peter? Why were you beating the crap out of Roger?"

"You don't know what he did, Chris," Dad said between sobs.

"What could he have done to cause you to do this? If I hadn't come in when I did, you could have killed him."

"No Chris, I WOULD have killed him."

"Why?"

Dad was able to stop crying enough to explain to Chris what happened.

"He used Emily's death behind my back to change Adam's mind about going to Ole Miss. He told Adam I couldn't afford to leave Inspiration, and that it would break my heart if he went that far away to school. Then he said something about Adam leaving the area where his mom is buried."

Chris looked over at Roger who was holding his head back with a towel on his nose to help stop the bleeding.

"You low life piece of crap. I should finish what Peter started, Roger. Why did you do that to Adam?"

"I didn't want Peter to leave. If he left, I would have to shut the place down."

CHAPTER 7

The next few days were stress filled. Dad and I talked about speaking with an attorney to see if we could reverse the signed Letter of Intent with the NCAA, but we knew that would be fruitless. Jeremiah had already taken my place as the Ole Miss quarterback of the future.

If I wanted play football that fall, it would be at Lee University.

If Dad wanted to perform in the area for some extra cash, it would be at Stick's.

Although Dad had complete disdain for Roger, he showed up at Stick's every weekend to play and sing. It wasn't in his master plan, but it was work. He never played a Saturday night during football season.

Dad never missed a game.

A funny thing happened during our first game my freshman year. We were losing midway through the third quarter and our head coach's young daughter was standing on the sideline beside her dad holding the cord for his headset. She tugged on his coat and said, "Dad, you've got the wrong quarterback in the game."

Our coach agreed, put me in, and we won the game.

+ + +

During my freshman year at Lee, I was fortunate enough to win Freshman of the Year in the conference as well as All-Conference Offensive Player of the year. I missed Player of the Year by two votes. I was beat out by a redshirt senior linebacker who went on to play arena football.

I received the same honors my sophomore year, and added the title of All-Conference Player of the Year. I was also recognized as an Honorable Mention All-American.

Jeremiah Clark had been doing well for himself and Ole Miss. He took his first snap as starting quarterback at Ole Miss during his second season after the starting quarterback was hurt during the third game of that season.

He was recognized as Second Team All-American. Many believed when I only got Honorable Mention, it was simply because, being from a small school, I wasn't able to play in front of many prime time TV audiences.

Roger's ploy from two years earlier was still impacting my career, and everybody knew it. In terms of the school, I absolutely loved Lee University. It was everything a student could hope for; Lee had strong academics and teachers who really cared about students, and the campus environment was incredible.

On the Friday night prior to my first game during my senior season, while playing a set at Stick's, Dad noticed a familiar face in the crowd. It was Jordan Cassidy, the ESPN analyst from National Signing Day. Dad quickly ended the set so he could say hello to him.

"Jordan, what brings you back to this neck of the woods? I know it's not the food here at Stick's."

"The same thing that brought me here the first time, your son. We want to do a special segment on Adam if you guys are willing. There's some talk about him and the Heisman."

"What kind of special?" Dad hesitated, "Wait, did you say Heisman?"

"Well, Peter, Adam has done some pretty amazing things that have gone unnoticed by much of the sports world, and we want to change that."

"Really?"

"Really. His numbers clearly show that he is a big-time quarterback, and the way you guys handled the situation around National Signing Day shows impeccable character. I just believe his story should be told. That is, if you guys are ready to tell it."

Dad paused, "Uh, well, let's at least talk about it.

"How about tomorrow morning for breakfast before the game?"

"Sounds good to me. Okay. Let's do it."

"I passed a coffee shop down the road. Let's meet there at 9:00 in the morning."

"Perfect, I'll see you there at 9:00."

Dad said he didn't sleep well that night. He was excited about what this might mean for my career, and he was torn between whether to tell me about it or wait and see what Jordan had to say first. He decided to wait.

+ + +

That morning, Dad made the usual game day breakfast for me as he had done for every Saturday home game: pancakes, sausage, three eggs over easy, two pieces of toast, and a large glass of OJ. It was my game day breakfast of choice.

"Morning, Dad."

"Morning, son. Ready to kick off a new season?"

"I sure am." I said with a smile. "I just believe something special will happen this year."

"Me too, son. Me too."

Dad could hardly hold his excitement.

"Hey Dad, why aren't you eating?"

"Oh, I'm going to meet an old friend for breakfast before the game."

"Oh really?" I said with a smirk. "What's her name?"

Dad had only been on a couple of dates during all this time since mom's death. Over the past four to five years, everybody had been encouraging him to go out, but he just couldn't bring himself to do it. The two times he did, he told me all he could think about was Mom.

"He's an old friend I haven't seen in years. You may see him after the game today."

"Okay, well, I gotta go. Coach wants me to give the pre-game speech to the team today so I want to get there a little early."

"Alright, I know you will fire them up. I'll be in my normal spot for kickoff."

"I know you will, Dad. See you there."

+ + +

Later, I eventually heard all about Dad's meeting with Jordan.

"You're here already, Jordan?"

"Absolutely. I wouldn't want to miss my meeting to discuss the biggest sports story of the year would I?"

"Biggest story of the year?" Dad asked with a bit of surprise in his voice.

"That's right, Peter, the biggest sports story of the year. I believe something special is going to happen with Adam this year. I've just got that feeling."

Dad was shocked, but it was a pleasant shock.

"Jordan, it's strange that you say that. Just this morning, Adam mentioned he felt this year could be special. What do you think is up with that, Jordan?"

"I'll tell you, Peter. What that man did... was his name Roger?"

"Yeah—Roger."

"What Roger did was wrong. I know Adam wanted to go to Ole Miss. I also know you wanted him to go there, but you weren't going to let him know how much you wanted him to go. I know you wanted him to go there even before he made his own choice. Then in jumps this Roger character, and Adam ends up going to Lee. What Roger did was horrible. But we both know God can turn bad to good. I just believe that is what's about to happen this year."

"I hope you are right, Jordan, if there is a God."

"Oh, there is a God, Peter. And I believe you are about to see something good happen out of this."

"We'll see. Now what about this special year you are talking about?"

"The way I see it, Peter, we've got six weeks to put the story together before Lee has an away game at Michigan. Then two weeks after that, they play at UCLA against the Bruins. We all know Lee scheduled two or three tough games per year for the purpose of making money. Although that's not a bad thing, I was just thinking what if... what if either one of those games is close. Or what if they actually won one of them?"

"Well, Jordan, at that point, I would believe there is a God."

They both laughed. But beneath the surface, they both knew it was possible. We had several senior starters on the team, and had been winning our games by rather large margins over the past couple of years. Just the year before, Alabama only beat us by three points with a game ending field goal in a high scoring game. The year before that, we only lost to USC by ten.

Jordan said, "Peter, it doesn't matter whether they win, or whether the games are even close. Adam's story needs to be told. It needs to be told because there are kids struggling all over the country who need a hero, someone to look up to, someone to give them hope for a better tomorrow. I just believe Adam is that guy."

"Then let's do it, Jordan. As long as Adam agrees."

"I wouldn't do it any other way, Peter. Let's go to the game and then take Adam for a HUGE steak somewhere after the game and talk about it."

"Well, I've never known Adam to turn down a steak. Do you have a ticket for the game?"

"I've got my press pass. That's all I need, brother. I'll see you there."

"Alright, see you there."

+ + +

Meanwhile, I was about to give the pre-game speech to the team. I had also been thinking a lot about all the "what ifs" since late summer workouts. I felt really good about our offense and was convinced the defense could at least slow down anybody in the country, even the big boys. As I walked into the locker room to give the pre-game speech and start my senior year, it was a little sad to think this was my final year to play college football.

The first thing I saw was a banner I had never seen before. It was a large banner in our school colors of navy blue and burgundy that read:

PRESS ON TOWARD THE GOAL FOR THE PRIZE.

That was part of my grandfather's favorite verse of scripture, Philippians 3:14: "*I press on toward the goal for the prize of the upward call of God in Christ Jesus.*"

Coach Jabes, our head coach at Lee, never seemed like a religious sort of guy, and he wasn't big on banners and quotes. He was just a simple X's and O's type football guy who still wrote on a chalkboard.

Every time he drew a play up on the board, we would cringe. He was just an old-school kind of guy who didn't believe we needed to be inspired to play. It was all business to him.

I didn't give the banner much more thought. I was focused on my speech, which needed rehearsing. It was game day and time to put my game face on and get ready for battle.

The opponent that day was the highly ranked cross-state rival Lewis Creek College.

Kickoff was set for 12:15 PM.

As the other team members arrived, they told me they saw a young girl standing outside the door of the locker room holding a football and a pen. She asked each player to sign the ball. One by one, the guys took the football and pen and signed the ball. Each one handed the ball off to the next player in line. She seemed to know every player by name, even the freshmen.

As each guy signed the ball, she crossed his name off a list in the team media guide she purchased earlier that morning. She had every name crossed off her list, every name but mine and Charlie Parker's.

Although she had made sure she was standing at the door early, before players usually arrived at the stadium, she didn't know that Charlie and I had arrived early that day, Charlie for some additional treatment by the physical therapy staff, and I to practice my pre-game speech.

She knocked on the door of the locker room.

Nobody came.

She knocked harder.

Still nobody came.

She was about to give up when Thomas Alley, a senior linebacker who had heard her knocking, opened the door.

"Can I help you?" Thomas asked, softening his voice when he saw it was the little girl.

"I missed getting Charlie's and Adam's autographs. Can you help me?"

Thomas could see her holding the ball and pen, and remembered signing it for her earlier as he was walking in.

"You bet! Let me see your pen and that ball. I'll be right back—wait here."

Thomas found me first, and of course I signed it right away.

Charlie, on the other hand, had been in some pain and wasn't in the best of moods. Thomas approached Charlie while the trainers were finishing up.

"Charlie, can you sign this ball for a little girl who is waiting outside the locker room door? She said she has everyone's autograph but yours and Adam's. I just got Adam to sign it, so your autograph is the final one she needs."

"Are you *kidding* me? I'm not in the mood to sign a freakin' ball right now. I don't even know if I am going to get to play today or not. I've got more important things to do than sign a ball for some little girl."

Thomas knew not to argue with Charlie, especially when he was in one of his "Charlie Crazy" moods.

"Alright, have it your way."

Thomas took the pen and ball back to the door where the girl was patiently waiting. He thought about just handing her the ball as if he had both signatures, but couldn't do that to her.

"I'm sorry, but I couldn't get Charlie's signature right now. But I got Adam's, and he's the quarterback," as if that would cheer her up.

He expected her to be saddened by his inability to get Charlie to sign the ball, but what happened next surprised him.

Her smile blossomed into a big grin. "That's okay, Thomas. I know Charlie will want to sign this ball later." She turned and walked away with it under her arm.

Hearing about that little girl always reminds me of the impact we have off the field as well as on. I want to be worthy of signing some little girl's football. I never want to forget where I started and why I love the game.

+ + +

Coach Jabes came up to me and asked if I could take a rain check for giving the pre-game speech because he had something he wanted to say to the team. Of course I agreed. What else could I say?

Coach called the team together and gave the most inspiring pre-game speech I had ever heard. It centered on the theme of "Press on toward the goal for the prize." I'll never forget his words:

"Men, we are here today, not just to kick off another football season, but to kickoff something which will last forever. I am about to share something with you that can bring about a transformational shift in your thinking, something that can change the course of the rest of your life."

I had never heard him talk like that before.

He continued: "One year ago, a fourth of you were playing high school football. At the end of this season, a fourth of you will move on to the next phase of your life. This team, as it is today, will never play together again after this season. Today is the first game of the season for this team, a team that has never played a college football game together before. After today, there will never, ever, be a first game for this team again. After today, the events, stats, and score of this game will forever be packed away in the record books of college football. Everything you did, or didn't do to prepare for this game will impact what happens today. Everything you do, or don't do, today will impact where you will be, and what you will be able to accomplish tomorrow. That's just how it works. Minutes, hours, and days are made of moments, which are building blocks and great predictors for the future."

He looked around at the faces of every player on our team. Our eyes were all locked to his. Knowing we were with him 100%, he went on:

"Yesterday is gone. At this point you can't do anything but learn from it. So take what you can from yesterday, and *press on toward the goal for the prize*. Today is game day."

The room was silent except for the echo of his big voice.

"It's not game day because you have a game on the schedule for today. It's game day because EVERY day is game day. Right now is when all of the past culminates with present actions to forever change the future. Right now you must press on toward the goal for the prize."

Coach Jabes paused, and walked over to a table in the locker room. On top of the table was a box, and he reached inside the box and pulled out a football. It wasn't just any football, it was the one all of us had signed, everyone except Charlie.

Without saying a word, Coach Jabes walked around the locker room tossing the ball up into the air and catching it as he walked. Although it was only about a minute, it seemed like an eternity. I wondered what he was going to say next. Why is he just walking around tossing the ball up and catching it like that?

Then he abruptly stopped, about five feet from where I was standing. Looking straight at me, he said, "This is the ball every one of you signed..." He paused. "Everyone—except for you."

Just as I was about to speak up and declare I had signed the ball, I heard a voice from someone standing right behind me say,

"That's right, Coach." It was Charlie. "I...I didn't sign the ball because...well," Charlie stopped, and then said, "...because I made a mistake, Coach. Can I please sign the ball now?"

"Yes, Charlie, you may." Coach pulled the same pen from his pocket and handed the pen and the ball to Charlie who promptly signed the ball.

I'd swear Charlie had tears in his eyes as he took the Sharpie and scrawled his signature on the leather ball. Coach took the ball from Charlie and resumed his position in front of us all.

"Guys, you may not know this, but thirty years ago, my father-in-law was murdered at the store he owned. For years and years, we didn't know who did it. Then one day, twenty-three years later, we received a call letting us know there had been an arrest. It took two years for the case to work its way through the system to get to trial. But that day came. The prosecution and the defense pleaded their respective cases and the decision to convict or acquit was turned over to the jury to render their decision."

The silence was deafening. Finally, someone on the other side of the locker room asked, "What happened, Coach?"

Coach Jabes' voice sounded like a dry whisper. "He was convicted and sentenced to life in prison."

The same guy on the other side of the locker room asked, "How did they know he did it?"

Coach answered, "Because of DNA he left at the scene. There was a greater statistical chance that he was guilty than there are people on earth. One of the detectives told me they are working on technology that can pick up the smallest amounts of DNA. He told me they already know that we all leave DNA on everything we touch. For you guys, that now includes this football I am holding in my hand."

The room was totally quiet. After a brief pause, he said, "The DNA of this team is on this ball. It will be left on the field today, next week, and every game we play. The effects of the actions of the ones bearing that DNA will show up on the scoreboard and in the game summaries of every game."

He looked at Charlie.

"Charlie, before you signed this ball, it did not contain the full DNA of this team. It was incomplete. Each one of you had to hold the ball, and sign your name to it. Now it's complete. However, the question remains. Will the full DNA representing this team be on display on the field today, and next week, and the next week, and the next, throughout the season, as it is on this ball? Your DNA is basically your signature. It's with you everywhere you go. One day, God asked Moses: 'What is in your hand?' and Moses replied: 'A staff.' Today I am asking you: What is in your hand? What are you capable of doing? What are you guys holding onto together? What are you capable of doing together? What will the DNA of this team reveal as the season plays out? Are you willing to press on toward the goal for the prize? Are you willing to put your signature on what we accomplish this year?"

One player yelled out, "Yes sir." Everybody else just looked stunned.

Coach said it again, but slower, "Are you willing to put your DNA, your undeniable signature on what we accomplish this year?"

Others joined in, "Yes sir."

Again, in a slower and louder voice than before, Coach said, "Are you willing to put your DNA, your undeniable signature on what we accomplish this year?"

By now it was all of us, almost in a frenzy. "Yes, sir!"

Coach said, "Then get out there and do it!"

We all ran out of the locker room and onto the field where the stands were full with an overflow crowd standing along the fence between our sideline and the stadium seats.

After the game, Dad and I met with Jordan. We agreed. ESPN planned a story about me to air later in the season.

It was going to be a season to remember.

CHAPTER 8

By the end of that season, we were 11-1, losing our NCAA FCS Second Round playoff game in overtime against eventual National Champion, Liberty University. We had already beaten two Division I powerhouse teams that year, one in the Big 12 Conference, and one in the Pacific 12 Conference. We believed we were well on our way to winning the National Championship until we lost that game 59-58 in an epic battle. No one could deny, at our level over the past two years, we had been the best team in the nation until that one loss. There was some talk about what would happen if we were able to play in a major bowl game, but that wasn't in the realm of possibility. The major bowl game talk was just a distraction brought up by some blogger who made some great points. At least we thought they were great points.

We won the National Championship for our size school the year before. That year, I broke several quarterback records, including most touchdown passes, least interceptions, most rushing yards gained by a quarterback, most passing yards, and was awarded National Player of the Year. Like one of my favorite quarterbacks to watch, Marcus Mariota, I had been selected as the Polynesian College Football Player of the Year by the Polynesian Football Hall of Fame selection committee. That was special to me. There was also chatter going around about me being a finalist to attend the Heisman ceremony. The Heisman Trophy is the highest individual award given to a college football player. There were even some comparisons to Marcus. That in itself was enough for me.

The blogger generating all the conversation about what would happen if we went to a major bowl played a huge role, along with what Jordan did with ESPN, in the chatter about the Heisman. It all happened so fast. It was like a crazy dream for me. I couldn't believe it; I was invited to New York City as a Heisman finalist.

There were three finalists invited to the award ceremony in New York that year, which is the minimum that can be invited. There have been as many as eight. Just being invited as a finalist was a great honor. The other two were Carter Reese from USC, and Jeremiah Clark from Ole Miss. What concerned me the most was the thought of sitting there with the one person who was living out my dream. I loved Lee University, but my dream had been to play for Ole Miss.

+ + +

Without a playoff game to play in the week leading up to the Heisman award ceremony, there were no scheduling concerns as far as team meetings. But there was the issue of finding and buying a great suit to wear because I certainly didn't have one hanging in my closet. Fortunately, one of my dad's friends, Greg, from Dad's old record label, knew there were some financial concerns, and stepped in to help.

Greg took me to his friend's clothing store and bought the best suit hanging on the rack for me to wear in New York. Other than the fact we lost that playoff game, it was an incredible week.

The only thing left to do was for Elizabeth and me to ensure Dad would be at the airport and on the plane when it was time to go.

Dad never had been the best at being places on time. I guess that's just the life of an artist. The only thing I had seen him consistently being on time to was driving the school bus. He needed that job for us to survive.

On the night before we were scheduled to fly to New York, Elizabeth and I printed out our boarding passes for the flights and took Dad's to him. That night was some special night at Stick's and Dad was playing to a rather large crowd. I had never been inside Stick's when it was officially open.

I remember sitting outside in my old beat up Mustang convertible with Elizabeth that night. It was an unusually warm December night and I had the top down on the car. I had to park near the road because almost every parking spot was taken.

We were only there to give my dad his boarding pass. I knew he would be out late that night because of the event at Stick's and I had planned to stay on campus with a friend.

Although I'm not sure what it was, something made me just want to sit in the car and stare up at the sky. As I stared at the beautifully lit sky above, I could see more stars than I had ever seen before. It was such a clear night, and the only lights Stick's had were closer to the building. They were dim. The message on the arrow sign near the road read: "Peter Alford—These Ain't Raindrops" as if he were only a one-hit wonder.

Still, it was the stars that captured my attention that night. I just stared at the sky with a thousand thoughts racing through my mind: *Why am I here? What does the future look like for me? Will I win the Heisman? Will Dad make the flight to New York tomorrow? I wonder if Mom is looking down from Heaven and can see me?*

Elizabeth gently reached over and held my hand. Suddenly I had a peace. She was my rock. She was the one I could totally count on to be there. Dad tried, but there were times when I'm sure he was dealing with his own issues and, just wasn't completely there with me even when he was present. Elizabeth was always there.

She waited several minutes, allowing me to corral my thoughts, then said, "Adam, are you ready to give this boarding pass to your Dad?"

"Uh, yeah." But I kept staring at the sky.

The only thought that consumed me had to do with whether Mom could be looking down on me from Heaven. Man, I missed her all the time, but especially in moments like these. I kept staring at the stars.

"Adam, are you ready?" she gently asked me again.

"Yep, let's do this."

+ + +

We got out of the car and walked to the door at Stick's. Although I'm sure Roger was charging a cover that night, no one was standing at the door. So we just walked in.

The spotlight was on Dad, the crowd was engaged, and he was rockin' it with "Rock Children Rock," a song he wrote for his first album. It was one of the songs he was going to sing at the concert they had to cancel because of the storm. The crowd was into it and the place was electric. It surprised Elizabeth to some extent, although she didn't say anything about it that night.

We walked up close to the stage near Dad, but just off to the side of the spotlight. He didn't see us until after the end of the song when the spotlight was off and the house lights came up a bit. He was about to take a short break and that's when I could get his boarding pass to him.

"Alright, guys! Are you having a great time tonight at Stick's?"

Of course the crowd responded with cheers. I've been told they would cheer at anything he would say.

"The band and I are going to take a short break and we will be back up in fifteen."

At that point Dad looked over at me and motioned for Elizabeth and me to meet him backstage. It was just a section behind the stage that kept any well-meaning but overstepping fans at bay.

"What's up, Adam?

"Dad, Elizabeth and I brought your boarding pass for tomorrow's flight to New York for the Heisman ceremony."

"New York? We're flying to New York tomorrow?"

Okay, I was pretty sure he was kidding, but the way Dad was at the time, I wasn't totally sure.

"Dad…"

"Son, you are going to win the Heisman, and Elizabeth, her mom, and I will be right there with you when you give your speech. Look, you and Elizabeth meet me at the airport. I have a quick errand to run early in the morning but will meet you guys at the gate. Trust me, I'll be there."

I was relieved, but still not totally confident he would make it. As long as people were there buying drinks, Roger would keep Dad going, even if he had to play some of the same songs two or three times over and over.

"Alright, Dad, Elizabeth and I will meet you at the airport in the morning. Our flight leaves at 10:00. If you aren't there outside security by 9:00, we will go to the gate and wait for you there."

"Adam, I will be up and running before you and Elizabeth even wake up. So there is no way I will miss that flight."

I still had an uneasy feeling. But there was nothing else I could do.

"Okay, Dad, see you then."

"See you there, buddy."

Elizabeth and I made it back through the crowd near the stage and walked toward the door. Dad walked back on stage. He grabbed his guitar and started to re-tune it. By this time, he was getting back into performing and it even seemed to give him a new level of energy. It was like fifteen minutes was too long for a break.

When we got to the door, I turned around to get one last look at the stage before we walked out, and saw something that disturbed me.

Elizabeth could tell something was wrong with me.

"What is it, Adam?" She asked as she turned to look at the stage.

There Dad was, stooped down on the stage, holding his guitar and focused on some female fan who had captured his attention. She was a beautiful woman wearing a very low cut, short black dress.

Somehow I knew there would be a day Dad would be able to move on past the pain of losing Mom and find someone. But I knew this wasn't the time or the place. Not now, not some random fan, and certainly not here at Stick's.

Elizabeth asked again: "What is it, Adam?"

"He won't be there."

"Won't be where? Adam, what's wrong?"

"Dad won't be at the airport for the flight in the morning."

"How do you know?"

"Just look at him."

"Adam, he's just talking to some fan who probably just wants an autograph."

"No, she wants a lot more than his autograph."

"How can you say that, Adam? What makes you think that?"

"I don't know why, Elizabeth. I just know."

And that was it. We walked out the door, across the parking lot, got in the car and left. I believe Elizabeth knew there was no need in trying to talk to me about it. I was either right or wrong, and we wouldn't know until 10:00 the next morning.

+ + +

That night, I stayed at a friend's apartment near campus. I couldn't sleep much. Maybe it was because I was all keyed up over the trip to New York and the Heisman ceremony, maybe it was because I was concerned about Dad and that woman, or maybe it was just the pizza Elizabeth and I had for dinner way too late that night.

I tossed and turned in the bed all night. The one time I did actually drift off to sleep didn't last long because I was awakened by the sound of the sirens of several first responders racing toward some emergency. I knew I had dropped Elizabeth off at her house on the other side of town, so she was safe. I was concerned about Dad, then quickly realized wherever they were going was not toward our house or Stick's.

I tried to go back to sleep, but only dozed off a couple of times. The alarm went off and it was like I had just gone to sleep, which was probably the case. I got up, got ready and grabbed a cup of coffee. I was out of there in no time to pick Elizabeth up for the trip to the airport. Her mom was going to join us in New York, and she was scheduled to fly in on a later flight that day.

As I drove past our house on the way to Elizabeth's, I noticed Dad's truck was there. I wasn't surprised. He may have had good intentions, but I didn't really think he would be up early running an errand after a long night at Stick's. I just hoped he would be at the airport on time. To this day, I don't know why I didn't just call him or stop by to be sure he was awake, and I certainly had no idea what was about to transpire that day.

Elizabeth and I got to the airport and sailed through security while the lines were short, thinking we would meet Dad at the gate. Once we got through security, time seemed to slow down to a crawl. Seconds seemed like minutes and minutes seemed like hours.

Dad wasn't there yet. I tried his cell fifteen minutes before we were about to board the plane, hoping beyond hope he was just about to zip through security. No answer. It went straight to voice mail.

Ten minutes before boarding, I called again. Still no answer. Five minutes, same thing. By then, the gate agent began making announcements about the flight and explaining how we would board by zone numbers. Still no sign of Dad.

We boarded the plane, found our seats, and buckled in, still hoping Dad might show up. We didn't talk much. Elizabeth knew I was too stressed to talk. There really wasn't much to say. We were just waiting for Dad. There were several people on our flight who recognized me. A couple of kids asked for an autograph and I quickly smiled, greeted them, and signed whatever it was they handed me.

There was one older guy who wanted an autograph on some kind of special paper he was holding. I wondered if it were really for him or if he had plans to sell it. I had been warned about autograph seekers who always have a bag of memorabilia close by to get athletes to sign and then sell online. I just signed it and let him pass on by to his seat. My real concern was about my dad.

As the flight attendants were closing and latching the door so the plane could be pressurized, Elizabeth leaned over to me and said, "Maybe he can get on that flight with my mom. I'll call her after we land in New York."

"Yeah, maybe," were the only words I could muster.

This day was not starting out so well.

+ + +

As soon as we landed in New York, we both turned on our phones. I tried to call my dad. No answer. Elizabeth called her mom during our taxi to the gate. I was trying to think of who else I could call when Elizabeth said, "I just called my mom to ask her to check on your dad, but it went to voice mail."

That was all we could do at the time.

The plane taxied to the gate and we got off the plane with the hope that somehow we would find dad and get him on a later flight. Just as we walked past the gate agent, I was about to ask Elizabeth to call her mom again when I saw Jordan Cassidy, the ESPN analyst, waiting there.

We saw each other at the same time. He came up to me with a rather strange look on his face and said, "Adam, we need to talk. I've arranged with a friend for us to have a private room in the Delta Sky Club just across the way. We don't have to stop and check in. They know who we are, so we can go right in."

"What? What's going on, Jordan? Is this about the Heisman? Can Elizabeth come with us?"

"Yes, and yes. I mean no, and yes. Just come with me, Adam. You too, Elizabeth."

It was all happening so fast I couldn't think straight. No. Yes. I was stunned, baffled, whatever other words you want to include. I didn't know what else to ask or say, so Elizabeth and I just followed Jordan across and into the Delta Sky Club and into a private conference room.

Jordan began to speak:

"Adam, I don't know how to tell you this, but your dad…"

"My dad?"

I could hear Elizabeth gasp and say: "Oh my God."

"My dad, Jordan, what about my dad? Is he okay? He's not hurt is he? He's not…"

Jordan interrupted me because I needed to give him time to tell me what he was there to say.

"Adam, your dad is okay, but he's been arrested."

"*Arrested*? For what? Was he drinking again?" I looked over at Elizabeth. "I told you that woman was no good. I told you she was up to something. She got my dad drinking didn't she, Jordan? I just knew it."

"Adam," Jordan said in a calm voice, "we're going to get through this. Somehow we're going to get through this. This morning, your dad was arrested for something tied to a murder investigation."

"What? My dad would never."

"Adam, just hear me out. This is what we have to deal with. He may be as innocent as you and I. But he's been arrested and we have to deal with it."

"Then let's go back and get him out. Let's get right back on that plane and get him out. He doesn't belong behind bars. He didn't do anything. I just know it. He's my dad, Jordan, and I know he didn't do anything wrong."

Jordan said, "That's why we came in here, Adam. There's a lot of media out there who want to report on the story. Right now, you and your dad are the absolute hottest story, not only in sports news, but in all news. There will be reporters on the other side of security just there to do their jobs. This is news. It's big, big news. We just need to figure out the next steps and do what's best for you and for your dad."

"Jordan, you are media too. How did you get past security?"

"I booked the cheapest flight I could book just so I would have a boarding pass. That allowed me to get past security to be at the gate when you landed. I wanted to get to you before the other reporters."

Although that was smart on his part, it brought up another question.

"Is that why you are here? Is that why you are helping me? Just to get a story? Maybe Elizabeth and I should just walk right out of here, find the next flight home, and just take it. Elizabeth, have you called your mother yet?"

Before she could answer, Jordan said, "Adam, you know, if I just wanted a story about you, I would have published what I know from behind the scenes on National Signing Day when you were in high school. I didn't violate your trust then, and I won't now. You have to trust someone. I am here because I care."

"Jordan, what happened? Why are they saying my dad did this?"

"Let's take this one step at a time, Adam. First of all, Elizabeth," Jordan looked over at her. "I'm so glad you are here. Right now, you are the most important person in Adam's life. He needs you more now than he ever has."

"Yes, of course. I am 100% here to do whatever I can for Adam. I've got to tell my mom. She used to be the County Attorney General."

"Your mom already knows. When I heard about this, I was already here at the airport waiting, like the other reporters outside, to report on Adam landing. Adam was already the biggest story in sports today. There is a lot of chatter that he has a really good chance to win the Heisman because a lot of voters changed their minds at the last minute and not only voted for Adam, but started sharing that they voted for him."

I interrupted, "Jordan, I don't give a crap about the Heisman, football, or anything else right now. I just want to get back home, see my dad, and help get him free."

"Adam," there was something in Jordan's voice that was calming, "for the next 24-48 hours, your dad is going to be held for police interrogations. The only person he may be able to speak with during that time is an attorney. We can see what we can do to get you on a call with him. But seeing him right now would be next to impossible. What we've got to do is decide the best thing to do for you and your dad."

I couldn't believe this was happening. Of all days—surely Dad wouldn't do something like this. Something was terribly wrong.

+ + +

I came out of my daze and heard Jordan saying, "...and, Elizabeth, as I said your mom already knows. She was the person Adam's dad called. He remembered she had been an attorney and he thought he could trust her. Fortunately, as you know Elizabeth, because she was doing some pro-bono work for a few non-profits in the area, she had maintained her license to practice law. So she was able to speak with Peter as an attorney."

Jordan looked at me.

"He was very concerned about you and how this would impact you, Adam. He asked Elizabeth's mom to contact me with hope I could catch you, as I did, before the rest of the media had a chance to ask you questions about something you knew nothing about. He was afraid you would hear that from them and that is not what he wanted."

"So he is the reason you are here for me?"

"Yes, Adam. He trusts me and I am not going to let him down. The only reason you weren't bombarded by the media people who are out there now is because I was able to explain the situation to them and let them know that you would have no clue when you stepped off that plane. I asked them to allow me to tell you in private and they all agreed. They are good people, Adam. They're just trying to do their job. Now we have better control of the situation. We have a private place we can plan out our next steps."

"So what do we do now, Jordan? We can't just sit here."

"That's right, we can't, and we won't. We won't leave until we have a game plan in place. You know, Adam, just like you have before a game. It's all about the game plan."

"Okay, Jordan, let's do it. But what can you tell me about what happened?"

"Here's what we know right now, Adam. At some point after three this morning, a neighbor to a lady named Ashley Smith was awakened by a disturbance in or around Ashley's house where she lived alone. She said she heard what sounded like a woman scream. The police and EMT's were sent to her house when the neighbor called 911 after she saw a male leaving the house, seemingly in a hurry."

"But she said a male, not my dad."

"That's right, Adam, and that may be the key. Your dad was not identified as the person fleeing the house. The reason your dad was arrested is that he fought against the police when they came to question him about what happened to Ms. Smith at her house."

"So what happened?"

"The details are rather sketchy at this point, but I'll tell you what I know."

"Apparently someone murdered Ms. Smith in her house. There was no sign of breaking and entering. Your dad was the last person seen with her last night. He was seen by several witnesses leaving with Ms. Smith. It seems they had been somewhat of the discussion of patrons that night. Of course, you know everybody at Stick's knows your dad hasn't been dating anyone. So people noticed when he left at the same time she did."

Elizabeth and I looked at each other.

"I told you that lady would be trouble, Elizabeth."

Jordan interjected: "Adam, don't let yourself go there. This lady was murdered by someone last night. She is the victim here."

"Sorry, it's just that Dad…"

"I know, Adam. All we can do at this point is to let it play out. Meantime, we have to make some decisions concerning the Heisman ceremony."

"The Heisman ceremony? I don't care anything about that now, Jordan. I just want to be with my dad. And I'm not going to win anyway. I just want to go home."

"Elizabeth's mom told me you would say that, Adam."

"No disrespect, but how would she know that?"

"Well, Adam, first of all, that's what anyone who really loved their dad would want to do. But it was your dad who told her you would want to leave. The first thing he said to her when she walked in to represent him was, 'Don't let this cause Adam to miss the Heisman ceremony.' Then he asked her to call me. Like I said before, that's why I'm here."

"Are you saying my dad wants me to stay and attend the Heisman ceremony?"

"According to Elizabeth's mom, that's exactly what he wants."

"Why? Why would he want me to stay here?"

"Look at it this way, Adam, maybe your dad knows he is completely innocent and will walk away from this soon. Maybe he doesn't want you to miss out on one of the most important days of your life so far."

"But I don't want to be here without him."

"And he doesn't want you to miss it because he can't be here."

"I don't know what to do, Jordan. I don't want to be here, but I don't want to let my dad down if he wants me to attend the ceremony."

"So do you really want to leave right now, or honor your dad by doing what he thinks is best for you?"

"Well…" I paused. "When you put it like that, I don't really have a choice. I guess I'm staying. But will you promise to keep me up to date on everything as soon as you know it?"

"Yes, I will, Adam, and not only that, I am going to stay by your side the entire way through. I've already called my boss at ESPN and he completely understands. Obviously, we are going to cover the story, there's no way to ignore it. But he told me that he will put another reporter on the story and that I can keep what happens between you, me, and of course Elizabeth."

"He said that to you?"

"Adam, you know I told you this is the biggest story in the news right now, not just sports. But yes, we all understand and want to do our part to help you and your dad. I'm sure the other reporter is already out there with the media group, which I am sure is growing as we speak. That reporter will hear what we decide to share with the media."

"And you're sure I can't be with Dad right now?"

"I am positive about that. And I promise I will see if there is any way you can speak with him over the phone. Just don't hold your breath about that at this point. Plus, I will be speaking with Elizabeth's mom several times through the day. You know your Dad will want to know what you are doing and how things are going with you as much as you want to know about him."

"I guess. No, I know you are right, Jordan. Thank you for being here. I don't know what I would have done if I heard this from the media. It just wouldn't have been right, or fair. Will I have to do any interviews while I'm here?"

"We are going to avoid that as much as possible. For now, if you are caught by some overly aggressive reporter, just tell him or her that you believe in your dad, and that you are here because he wants you to be here. That should do it."

"If Dad isn't going to be here, and Elizabeth's mom isn't going to be here, where will we stay?"

"I've already thought about that, Adam. First of all, Elizabeth, if you want to go back, we can make arrangements for you to fly back today."

Elizabeth chimed in, "If there is any way for me to stay, I'm staying. I want to be here for Adam."

"Okay, that's what I thought you would want to do. So did your mom. So here's the plan. It's probably best that we stay somewhere different from where you guys were going to stay. At least for a while, that will give us a chance for some privacy as things are getting worked out back in Inspiration. I have decided that I am not going to be involved with reporting this story. At this point, I am just a friend of your dad's and Elizabeth's mom. When I was speaking with Elizabeth's mom, she brought up the question of where you guys would stay. She asked where would be the best place to stay to avoid as much media attention as possible. I told her and she has already booked your rooms there. I booked mine."

I took a deep breath. My head was spinning. There was so much going on. I wanted to run. I wanted to run home to Dad. I wanted to run away from it all. I don't know what I would have done had Elizabeth not been there, and if Jordan hadn't been there to take such good care of us. With all this going on, I'm sure it would have turned into an even bigger three-ring circus.

From what I had heard, the Heisman ceremony can turn into a media frenzy. I had mixed feelings about staying, but staying just felt right because that's what my dad wanted. We found a way to get out of the airport, past the media, and to the hotel.

CHAPTER 9

I made the decision to stay for the time being, but there were still a few things on my mind. The first and foremost was when I could speak with my dad. I just knew he was innocent. I also knew I wouldn't get to speak with him much, until the ceremony was over. Although he wasn't arrested for murder, as Jordan said, he was arrested. That confused me. So I asked, "Jordan, can you explain exactly why my dad was arrested? Why was he fighting against the police?"

"I don't know all of the details, Adam, because I have been working on making sure you are taken care of first. But, I have sources who told me they believe he was arrested because when the police arrived at his house to speak with him about the situation concerning Ms. Smith, he told them he couldn't take time to talk to them because he needed to get to the airport. It must have been pretty rough because they had to restrain him. I believe he pushed an officer down."

Dad had always been a fan of law enforcement and was friends with most of the officers in town. So they all knew him. I couldn't imagine him pushing an officer.

During a call he was allowed to make to me later from the county jail, he explained what happened. He told me he met Ashley that night and confirmed that was the lady Elizabeth and I saw him talking to when we left. He said she was beautiful and seemed like a sweet lady. She told him she was a songwriter and told him that night she wanted him to hear some of her music.

He said he knows it sounds kind of cheesy and looks bad for him, but he truly just wanted to help her with her music. He said they talked quite a bit that night and he could tell she knew her stuff when it came to writing. He said writers just know when someone else is an authentic writer or when that person is just a 'wanna be' writer. Dad thought she was the real deal.

So he did something he had never done before. He let her take the mic and sing. He didn't even ask Roger. What was Roger going to do anyway, fire him?

Dad said she absolutely nailed it. She performed one of the songs she wrote and he loved the song and her voice. He told me he was kind of interested in her. I never heard dad talk about a woman like that other than Mom. I wasn't sure if he meant interested in her talent, or specifically interested in her. I wanted to know more. So I asked, "What happened next, Dad?"

"I don't know, Adam. It was weird. It was like we were already close friends but we had only met that night. I guess music can do that to you."

"So you left with her?"

"Yeah, but it's not what you think. Sure, she was beautiful, but nothing happened between us."

"Where did you go when you left?"

"We went to her house."

"To her house? Really, Dad?"

"She told me she didn't normally stay out that late and that she was a little nervous going home by herself."

"And you bought that?"

"I did. And I do now more than ever."

"What do you mean?"

"She told me she had a strange feeling someone had been snooping around her house. She even thinks the person tried to get in one night while she was sleeping."

"Really?"

"Yeah, she said she didn't report it because she couldn't prove anything. But she just knew, and was concerned going in that late at night. So I told her I would follow her home and go through her house with her."

"Well, she must not have been too afraid if she let a stranger follow her home and then go through her house. After all, she just met you that night. Right?"

"Right. She must have felt the same connection to me that I felt with her. Music is a funny thing, son. Plus, she knew about me. She knew who I was, and she knew the story about your mom. I guess she just trusted me."

"I guess."

"You know. If I had not followed her home, and had not gone through her house with her that night, I would have never been questioned, or arrested, and I would have been in New York with you."

"I know. I bet you wished you had never gone in her house."

"I'm not so sure, Adam."

"What? Now I'm really confused."

"Adam, what happened to her could have happened anyway, so I'm not sure I helped, other than the fact she wasn't afraid when I was there.

But, had I not followed her home, and had not gone through the house with her that night, I would have probably blamed myself for the rest of my life. I would have heard her voice over and over telling me she was nervous about going home by herself and going in that house. At least this way, I'm not fighting that internal battle. I did my part, and would do it all over again. I just wish I could have been there to stop what happened."

"I guess. So why were you arrested?"

"Well, that's where I messed up. That one is all on me."

"What did you do?"

"It was really late when I got home, I hadn't packed for the trip yet, and I knew I needed to get that done before I went to sleep. There was nothing that was going to stop me from being at the airport to meet you guys. At least that's what I thought."

"Yeah, me too."

Dad continued, "I packed, put my bag by the door and fell asleep on the couch. I had strained my back a little during my performance earlier that night, but took something for it and went right to sleep. I was sleeping so sound I didn't hear my alarm going off. What woke me up was the officers banging on my door."

Dad paused and swallowed hard, remembering how it happened. "I opened the door and two officers came in. I was still sleepy and not everything was registering with me. They started questioning me about Ashley, where we went when we left Stick's, and when was the last time I saw her. I didn't have a clue why they were there or what was going on. At some point, I realized I was about to be late to the airport and just walked over to the door, picked up my bag, and told them I had no clue what they were talking about, but I had to catch a flight."

He tried to laugh. "Just as I started to open the door, one of the younger officers stepped in front of me, grabbed my arm and said, 'Sir, you aren't going anywhere until we say you can go.' That's when it got a little rough. I said something I shouldn't have said, then pushed the officer away from me, and opened the door. The other officer threw me down, shoved my face on the floor, and cuffed me. It was all downhill from there."

"I don't know what to say, Dad. Can you fly up in the morning so you can be here in time?"

"I don't think so, Son. I know what I did was stupid. But I did it and here I am."

"Then I'm flying home. Forget the Heisman ceremony. I just don't care anymore."

"Don't say that, Son. You've earned this and you should stay for it. That's why we reached out to Jordan, and he agreed to be there for you and help. I really want you to stay."

"Dad, I'm not going to win anyway. Why does it matter?"

"I can't explain why, Adam, but I can tell you it matters." He paused and played his ace in the hole: "I know your mother would want you to be there."

"Dad, don't…"

"Just stay, okay?" he pleaded. "There's nothing you can do here right now—just stay for me."

"Okay, I love you, Dad. Good bye."

Looking over at Jordan, I said, "Okay, I'm staying, but I need you to be right here and walk me through this cause I'm pretty confused right now."

He looked back at me, took a breath, and said, "Someday you will thank your dad for getting you to stay."

I put my hand on his shoulder and said, "And today, I am thanking you for helping me get through this mess."

"Great then, Adam. Let's get to work on your speech."

"My speech?"

"Yeah, what you will say when you win."

"You mean *if* I win—which we both know is more than a long shot. I'm just here because my dad wants me to be here, and it makes for a good story with a kid from a very small school being a finalist. I feel I owe it to my team, and Coach Jabes, who is home with his wife who just had surgery on her foot."

Without a blink, Jordan said, "But what if you do?"

CHAPTER 10

New York City never sleeps and there's always something to do. Add to that being a finalist for the Heisman, and things got pretty interesting. The fact that Dad had been arrested made everything more intense. I tried not to watch the news and tried to lay low. I stayed away from all social media.

Jordan helped me navigate the process. He helped me understand the media and why certain questions would be asked. He gave me advice on the questions to answer and how to respond politely to the ones I didn't need to answer. He helped me understand that, although many of the questions and the way they were asked upset me, no one intended to hurt me. They were just trying to find an angle or way to get me to respond. There was nothing about it that was personal; and yet, it was all personal to me.

There were many times I was so hurt on the inside that I wanted to lash out at the person asking the question. There were times I wanted to just run away, and many times, I just wanted to cry.

I did kind of break down that night when no one except Jordan and Elizabeth were with me. I totally trusted them and knew they both cared about me.

I knew Elizabeth was the one I would want to be with for the rest of my life. I liked having Jordan's counsel, but knew that after this weekend, he had to go back to his analyst's job at ESPN. I remember thinking maybe he could be my agent. Although I already had some of the best agents in the business contacting me, I hadn't settled on one yet. There was no doubt I would need one soon.

On the morning of the award ceremony, there wasn't a lot to do. Jordan was able to get us out of the hotel without being seen and into a private area of a great restaurant. We made it back to the hotel without bumping into any media and I was able to get a little rest before getting ready to go on stage.

When it was time to go, I put on the sharpest suit I had ever worn in my life, a blue pinstripe, and felt like a million bucks. Almost everything I had on was either given to me or borrowed, even the watch—a shiny new Breitling Chronomat. That watch was sweet. Dad still had a lot of friends in the music industry, and they were doing what they could to help. I felt great, but I was missing Dad, Elizabeth's mom, and of course my mom.

I wondered if Dad was going to be able to watch the ceremony, but I didn't ask because I didn't want to know if the answer would be anything but yes. So I just went through the process and hoped he could watch.

Walking out the door, Jordan asked if I had the acceptance speech he helped me write. Of course I had it. I knew he wouldn't let me leave the hotel without it, so I had already printed it out and placed it in the pocket of my suit jacket.

It was a short ride to the venue. When we got there, we were ushered in through a back door and into a green room. The other finalists were there. The first one I saw was Carter Reese from USC.

"What's up, Adam?"

We had connected a few times after the announcement of the finalists. He was a great guy. I called him Hollywood because he was from Southern California.

"What's up, Hollywood?"

"Dude, I am so sorry to hear about your dad. I'm sure it will all work out."

If anyone else said that, I would have been pretty upset, but Carter was cool. I knew he meant it from his heart.

"I know, man. It's a bummer. I wish he could be here."

"I get it man. I wish my dad could be here too but he had a massive heart attack and died before I got out of high school."

"Oh my gosh, bro. I'm so sorry, I didn't know."

"It's alright, man. I'm sure he's looking down from Heaven."

Right then I realized that at least I would get to see my dad when I got back. But it also made me think about mom.

"Same with my mom, bro. She's probably standing right there by your dad looking down to watch."

"So I wonder which one has more pull with God?" Carter said to lighten the mood a bit.

"Pull with God?"

"Yeah, you know they both want their own son to win."

"Oh, I don't know man, maybe it will be a tie." We both laughed.

Of course there was one other finalist in the mix, Jeremiah Clark, the Ole Miss quarterback who had just walked back into the green room.

"Hey, Adam." Jeremiah said as he walked up.

"What's up, Jeremiah?"

We did a quick bro hug, and that was it.

It seemed a little awkward and I wasn't sure why. We just didn't have much to say to each other. He lived my college dream. He knew I had been Ole Miss' first choice until I backed out, and there we were, both about to walk out and be seated as Heisman finalists.

It wasn't that we didn't like each other. We really did. It was just awkward—being pitted against each other without being able to be on the field to determine who wins. The time finally came, and the production assistants ushered us to our seats. There were cameras everywhere utilizing every possible angle in the room.

It was show time.

+ + +

We were all called up to the stage to stand by the trophy.

To my surprise, Jordan was the ESPN guy who walked out on the stage to speak with us and lead up to the announcement of the winner. Later, he told me while we were in the green room, the person who was scheduled to be there had to leave at the last minute for a family emergency. Jordan was the only one there who didn't already have an assignment. He was just the logical choice.

Jordan cracked a few jokes with us to lighten up the evening.

He mentioned the fact that it was the first time for Jeremiah and me to be in New York and asked what we thought about it. Jeremiah mentioned he had been to the Statute of Liberty, and I said something about there being great food and that I wanted to visit Ground Zero before I left town.

He asked Carter if he had given us a tour of the city because it was his third time to visit. He said the first two were family vacations when he was a child and so he didn't want to get either of us lost. We all chuckled. It was probably more nervous laughter than really thinking it was funny.

We tried to seem as loose as we could, but after all, this was the Heisman ceremony. It's the biggest individual award in college football, and it was down to the three of us. Jordan did a great job, but we were all still uptight and ready for it to all be over, one way or the other.

Almost all living previous winners were there. Because I always wanted to be a quarterback, they were the ones I recognized the most. I saw Roger Staubach (who was my dad's favorite when he was young), and my favorite of all time, Marcus Mariota. It was like a fraternity, one I wanted to join, but one I thought I would never be part of because I went to such a small school.

We went to a short commercial break. During the commercial, the previous winners who were present were standing on stage just chatting. When it was time, the person in charge yelled for silence.

"And now we're back. It's time for the historic and life-changing handoff of the most prestigious individual award in college football, the Heisman Trophy. Please help me welcome…" and he introduced the person from the Heisman Trust who would be announcing the winner. They shook hands and Jordan walked off stage.

"Thank you, Jordan, for stepping in at the last minute, and for doing such a great job hosting the telecast this evening."

He didn't waste any time. He jumped right in to it.

"On behalf of the Heisman Trust, I would like to welcome the many fans present here with us tonight, and to the millions of fans watching with us across the country and around the world. This trophy recognizes the outstanding college football player whose performance best exhibits the pursuit of excellence with integrity. As reflected in our mission statement, winners epitomize great ability combined with diligence, perseverance, and hard work. This year, the Heisman Trust, with the assistance of our loyal sponsors, and the former winners here behind me tonight, have provided over $2 million dollars to deserving charities. But tonight, we are here to award the Heisman Trophy to one of these fine young men whose highlights on the field, and personal character on and off the field, clearly show why they are among the finalists."

He looked directly at us, as we were seated in front of the podium, and continued,

"Gentlemen, you are finalists based solely on your outstanding accomplishments this year. Your presence here tonight is a credit to many people, including your families, others who have helped you along the way, the schools you attend, your coaches, and your teammates. While only one of you will walk away tonight as a Heisman Trophy winner, you are all winners in life and on the football field. And now," he opened the envelope, "this year's winner of the Heisman Memorial Trophy is..."

He paused, smiled, looked right at me and said, "Adam Alford—from Lee University."

+ + +

I heard the applause. Everyone was standing. But I couldn't move.

I sat there in disbelief. The applause grew louder.

Jeremiah grabbed my hand and pulled me up. "You won, dude! You won the Heisman." And he hugged me.

I was still stunned. I didn't know what to do.

Carter pulled me in close, hugged me and said, "Go get your trophy, brother. You deserve it."

I walked up onto the stage, shook hands with the gentleman who announced me as the winner, and faced the crowd that was still standing and clapping. I could see Jordan and Elizabeth over to my right. I'll always remember the looks on their faces. The whole experience felt surreal.

I wiped the tears from my eyes and started to talk, completely forgetting about the speech I had printed out and put in my jacket. "Thank you. Thank you to the Heisman Trust for making this night possible. I am humbled and honored to be part of this organization which has helped so many children, veterans and others for so many years."

I paused to catch my breath before continuing, "Hotty Toddy, Jeremiah!"—this is how Ole Miss fans greet one another—"it has been a pleasure being here tonight with you and Carter, and I wish you both continued success on and off the field. Thank you to my teachers, teammates, my coaches at Lee University, and to Lee University President Dr. Paul Conn. I love every one of you and am grateful for all the experiences. Coach Jabes, you took me in at the last minute on National Signing Day and you have taught me so much about this game of football, and the game of life over the past four years. Thank you, and Go Flames! Thank you to my hometown of Inspiration, and the community of Cleveland, Tennessee for all you guys have done for me throughout the years. Finally, mom..."

I took a deep breath and continued, "Mom, I know you are in Heaven, and I hope you are looking down on your little boy. I've grown into a man now. I really did become a quarterback, and these very kind people have bestowed upon me an honor that I only dreamed was possible. I remember pretending doing the Heisman pose as a child playing football in the backyard. At the time, it was only a dream. Many times you saw me pretend I was giving a speech to accept this award. This time it's not play. It's real. Thank you for all you taught me while I had you. I hope I have become the man you wanted me to be. I miss you, Mom, and I wish you were here with me tonight."

I paused, wiped away tears, took a deep breath, looked straight into the camera lens, and continued,

"Dad, for so many years, all we had was each other. Thank you for everything you have taught me along the way. Thank you for being there for me and with me. Thank you for the sacrifices you made over and over again, just for me. I didn't want to come tonight without you, but you wanted me to be here. So I am here because of you. Not just because you wanted me to be here when I wanted to get right back on that plane and come back to where you are now, but I am here because of your teaching, your love, and the wisdom you have shared with me for all these years. I don't understand why you are where you are right now, but I do believe that you will be free soon, and this misunderstanding will be over soon. Thank you, Dad. Thank you for who you are, and thank you for the man you have helped, and are helping me to become."

I swallowed hard and wondered how long I had been talking. "Finally, I can't walk off this stage without mentioning the love of my life, Elizabeth. You know what you mean to me, and you know what I mean when I say there are no words to describe the love I have for you and that I know you have for me. Thank you for sticking by me, encouraging me, and even giving me some quarterbacking advice from time to time."

I thought I was finished, and turned around to shake hands with all of the previous Heisman winners standing behind me. Then I thought about Jordan and what he did for me. I turned back to the podium and said, "There's one more thing. Jordan Cassidy has been there for me on two separate occasions during my career. He is not only my all-time favorite analyst at ESPN, I consider him a mentor and a friend. Thank you, Jordan."

That was it, I turned back to the previous winners standing behind me, finished shaking hands with those I had missed before, and the biggest night of my life so far came to an end.

CHAPTER 11

The next day, Jordan dropped us off at the airport. I thanked him for his help, and we flew back home. Other than the fact that my dad was sitting in a county jail because of a temporary lapse in judgment in the heat of the moment, I should have been the happiest person on earth. After all, our best guess was that he would be released once they got everything sorted out and Elizabeth's mom did her legal thing. We thought he might get a slap on the wrist and that would be it. The problem was, I wasn't happy.

I'm not sure if it was that I missed my mom, because of all the stress or what, but I really struggled after being awarded the Heisman. At first, nobody but Elizabeth, her mom, and Jordan really knew what was going on. Somehow I was able to hide it from Dad. At first, it was pretty much just inside stuff, which didn't show to anyone who wasn't physically close to me. The reason I was able to hide it from Dad was because he didn't get out like we thought he would.

Things weren't going well. While Elizabeth's mom was working on getting him out, the investigators started thinking he may have been involved with the murder itself. In their minds the facts were straightforward. Witnesses saw them leave together the night she was killed. Dad did go to her house that night to be sure she made it home safely. He did go in and went through the house with her, so naturally his DNA could be found in the house. While this was clearly circumstantial evidence, the prosecutors believed their forensic evidence was a smoking gun.

But my dad wasn't capable of murder.

+ + +

According to Dad, while he was at Ashley's house that night, he had complained about straining his back on stage during the performance. Ashley picked up a prescription bottle of a mild painkiller and told dad there was only one pill left, and he could have it. She said the dentist had given it to her after she had some dental work done and it had just been sitting in her cabinet for a few weeks. She told him she had thought about throwing it away because she didn't need it, but hadn't yet. She told him to just toss the bottle when he finished. Although it was another momentary lapse in judgment, he took the pill bottle with him, and that was what he took that night.

After he took the pill, he had left the bottle on the coffee table in front of the sofa where he had fallen asleep. One of the officers discovered it while another officer was questioning Dad about the night before. They didn't say anything to him about it until later. Apparently the reason he over slept and was in such a hurry to get to the airport was because of the reaction he had to the pill.

While going through further interrogation, they asked dad if Ashley had ever been to our house. Of course he said no, because she hadn't. Then they asked if he had a prescription for Vicodin. Again, he replied no, because he didn't. What Dad didn't realize until later, was that they were forming a fairly strong case against him based on what they knew.

He said it all clicked in his mind when he remembered they had asked him if he would take a blood test shortly after they booked him. Dad realized they wanted to see if he had Vicodin or anything else in his system. The circumstantial evidence was that he was the last person seen with her that night. They could prove he had been in her house. It appeared someone had gone through the medicine cabinet in her master bathroom because the door to the cabinet had been left open, and some non-prescription bottles such as aspirin, were found in the sink. Her prescription bottle for Vicodin was found in Dad's possession, and Vicodin (for which he did not have a prescription) was in his system. One thing added to another, and the DA agreed to file formal charges against him for the murder of Ashley Smith.

Dad needed Elizabeth's mom, Bethany, more than ever. As I mentioned before, he trusted her, as did I, and knew she would do everything in her power to make sure the truth came out.

+ + +

It didn't look good for Dad.

"Adam, Elizabeth," Bethany paused. "I'm afraid I have bad news."

My heart sank. This wasn't good. We had been waiting to hear from her all day, but this was not what I was hoping to hear. Maybe it was just going to take longer to get my dad out of jail and get the charges dropped.

"Bad news about what?" Elizabeth asked.

She sighed. "Adam, your dad is in serious trouble."

"Serious trouble? What do you mean?"

Of course I already knew he had been in trouble, but at this point everything was racing through my mind.

"Did he get into a fight at the jail?"

"No, they are basically keeping him in a cell by himself, Adam. The D.A. just told me they are going to file formal charges against your dad tomorrow morning for the murder of Ashley Smith. They are also going to add burglary, and being in possession of a controlled substance. It appears they may charge him with felony murder."

"Hold on now, Bethany…"

"Adam, this is my mom—she's just trying to help," Elizabeth said with some concern in her voice. She could tell I was very agitated.

"I'm sorry." Then I addressed Elizabeth's mom, "Forgive me, Ms. Bethany—I'm just upset. This whole thing…"

"I know, Adam. I don't believe your dad did anything wrong. I can't prove that yet, but I believe I can later. Right now, we just have to deal with the situation at hand and take this one step at a time."

"I thought that's what we were doing before. Now look at where we are."

"The best thing for you to do, Adam, is to pray for your dad, and pray that somehow I can figure this out. Right now, it looks pretty bad. Is there anywhere you can go for a few days? Do you have any family living in another area?"

"No ma'am. You know my grandparents were killed in that storm with my mom when I was ten, and Dad's parents passed away a long time ago. We just haven't been close to anyone else in the family."

"What about Roger? I know your dad worked for him for a long time."

"No way. It's his fault I didn't go to Ole Miss. No way I'm ever asking him for anything."

"You are more than welcome to stay here, but with me representing your dad, that could create some unwanted media attention. My total focus has got to be on this situation with your dad."

"The only two other people I can think of are dad's old drummer George and his wife Kim. But Kim has recently been sick with something, and I just don't feel comfortable calling and asking them."

Elizabeth chimed in, "I have an idea. Let me make a call."

She stepped away for about five minutes and then came back.

"How would you feel about staying with Jordan?"

"Jordan from ESPN?"

"Yes. He gave me his cell number while we were in New York and asked me not to hesitate to call if we needed him for anything. So I just called him and he said he and his wife would love to help out. In fact, he said they had just moved and renovated an area above their garage in Irvine. He said it's like a nice apartment and would be perfect for you. He also said there is a really nice gym close by where you can work out."

"But doesn't Dad need me here?"

"Adam, your dad needs you to focus on the next steps in your life. He wants you focused on getting ready for the draft. There is nothing you can do for him here, and I promise I will call you every day with updates. I will do everything I can to get you two back together soon."

"Elizabeth? What about you—and us?"

"Adam, it's fine. We're good. Maybe I can do something to help my mom help your dad."

Bethany chimed in. "That's right, Elizabeth, there are some things I am going to need as we work through this, and I know you would be a big help."

"Okay, are you sure Jordan said that's fine with them?"

"Totally sure."

With that, we began making preparations for me to move to Irvine, California, to stay with Jordan and his wife.

CHAPTER 12

I rvine was a nice place. But it wasn't home.

Jordan was a great friend. But he wasn't my dad.

His wife, Jennifer, was an awesome hostess and a great cook. But I still felt depressed.

All I wanted was my dad back. Nothing else mattered. I left the Heisman trophy at Elizabeth's house, and I didn't really care about working out for the draft. All of my dreams about being an NFL quarterback were like a winding road in the rear view mirror. One more curve and there was nothing to see.

I was basically just going through the motions.

I went to the gym a lot. There were a few people who noticed me as the quarterback from the small school who won the Heisman, but they were all cool with it. There were very few questions.

Apparently the news about my dad was old news by now, or they were just respecting my privacy. I was basically just able to walk in, work out at my own pace, and just keep to myself the rest of the time.

There were several agents trying to connect with me to sign with them, but nobody really stuck out. They seemed okay, but I guess I just wasn't in the mood to make a decision like that at the time.

I received an invitation to play in the Senior Bowl in Mobile, Alabama, in January. That was very cool. I liked that we would be coached by an NFL coaching staff. I thought that would be beneficial. But I was concerned about facing the teams and media. I also wasn't too keen on the idea of going out and having fun with football while Dad was locked up in jail facing a murder charge. I just wanted to be back with him.

Jordan said if I wanted to play in the Senior Bowl, he thought it would actually be good for my dad to know I was working toward my dream and that his situation had not derailed my focus. He said although there would be a lot of sports media present, most of the scheduled interviews would be with ESPN and NFL Network where Jordan had some close friends. He believed they would not be too hard on me and he asked me to trust him and consider it.

+ + +

Although I wasn't able to call Dad, he called me about twice per week. We talked as long as they would allow him to stay on the phone. Each time, he encouraged me to stick with the workouts and to make a decision concerning an agent. He told me he wanted me to play in the Senior Bowl. It was like he had been talking with Jordan.

I told him I wasn't sure what to do about an agent. He said something that made me think. He asked if I had considered Jordan as my agent. Then he told me he didn't know very much about football agents and kidded that he would be able to help me if I could sing and play guitar.

It made me feel better that he could still joke around like that at times.

He never let me know he was struggling, but I know he had to be. He was locked up and charged with killing someone. Somehow we never really talked about the case. I don't believe he wanted to take our time to talk about it. Besides, Elizabeth and her mom were keeping me posted on developments every day there was something to share. Most of the time it was just that there was nothing new to discuss. There was a time when I just resigned myself to the fact that it was going to go to trial, and that's when Dad would be exonerated. I hated the wait, but there was nothing else I could do.

+ + +

Because Jordan had been traveling a lot with ESPN, he had racked up a ton of miles with Delta Airlines. He was very generous in telling me I could use his miles to fly back home to see Dad. I wanted to see my dad, but not locked up. I believe Dad felt the same way. We never actually said it to one another, but we both just knew. It wasn't ideal, but as long as we could talk on the phone, we were fine for the time being.

I had to make a decision about the Senior Bowl. I knew Dad wanted me to play, so I asked Jordan again about the media. Jordan seemed to always know the right thing to say.

"Come on, Adam. We are going to meet some of my friends at NFL Network."

"Huh?"

"You want to know about some of the media who will be at the Senior Bowl?"

"Uh, yeah."

"Then there is no better way to do that than to meet some of the guys that will be there. Come on, let's go."

I followed him to his car, where we got in and were on our way."

NFL Network is in Culver City, California, a suburb of Los Angeles, and only about forty-five miles from Irvine.

Jordan navigated traffic and people like a pro. He knew shortcuts to avoid traffic and called somebody named Justin at NFL Network while we were on the road. Not that I was eavesdropping, but he had the call on Bluetooth coming through the car's speakers. So obviously I could hear both ends of the conversation.

"Hey, Justin, what's up?"

"Jordan. How are you man?"

"I'm good. I got you on speaker here with my friend Adam Alford. Hey, are you guys good with me bringing him in today?"

"Anytime for you, Jordan. What's up, Adam?"

"Hey, Justin…"

Jordan spoke up, "We need to keep this visit low key, Justin. Is that cool?"

"Absolutely. But why do we need to keep it low key?"

"The reason I want to bring Adam over there is for him to meet you guys, and show him how solid you are. He is concerned about the media exposure, questions, etc. surrounding his dad's arrest if he plays in the Senior Bowl. I told him the media exposure would mostly be with NFL Network and that I wanted him to hear how you guys will interview him."

"Absolutely. Bring him in. Just let me know when you get here."

"Will do." said Jordan before ending the call.

"How do you do that, Jordan?"

"Do what?"

"You must know everybody in the sports world."

"Not everybody, but I do know a lot of people affiliated with football. You know, it's kind of my job to be involved in that circle."

"Apparently."

After a few minutes of just enjoying the ride, we arrived at NFL Network. Jordan was right. I met some good people there. Although my situation was big news, they just didn't ask, probably because they were abiding by Jordan's wishes.

After a couple of hours, we hit the road back to Irvine. As we were driving, Dad's words from our recent call kept coming back, 'Have you considered Jordan could be your agent?' So I just had to ask, "Jordan, could you be my agent?"

"Me, as your agent? Why me?"

"Jordan, I trust my dad, and I have learned to trust you. The other day, my dad asked if I had considered you as my agent."

"Well, Adam, I'm flattered. Almost every agent in the country wants to represent you."

"There are a lot of agents who would like to represent me. But I have to be with someone I completely trust. It's hard, and it takes time to learn who you can trust. Next to my dad, Elizabeth, and her mom, I trust you. So, will you?"

"There is a lot to think about there, Adam. Can we put that on pause and make sure you are set to play in the Senior Bowl first?"

"Sure."

+ + +

I asked Jordan one day what made him tick. He said, "One of my core convictions is found in a really old book. It goes like this, 'Do nothing out of selfish ambition or vain conceit. Rather, in humility value others above yourselves.' That's how I try to live my life." I had heard that before from my mom.

There was just something about Jordan. He reminded me a lot of my dad the way he cared for people and had a good heart. After he helped me get everything completed to attend the Senior Bowl, I brought up the issue of representation again.

"So tell me again, Adam, why do you want me to be your agent?"

"I trust you, Jordan. Your heart is in the right place. That's why I want you as my agent."

"I need to tell you something, Adam. Another one of my core convictions is that I want to have uncommon influence on people I meet and work with every day. About a year ago, I decided one way I could do that would be to become an agent and help guide young men like you into and throughout their career in professional sports, mainly football. I have had conversations with the people I report to at ESPN, and although they have said they don't want to lose me as an analyst, they understand me and want to support me any way they can. This past July, I successfully completed the examination, which was the final requirement to be a certified agent by the NFL Players Association. I had no intention of you being the first person I would represent. I really wanted to help you and your dad during this trying time in your lives. My plan was to get more organized and start next year. I guess this would speed up that plan."

"So you will do it?"

"Yes, I'll do it, Adam."

+ + +

There was a lot to do. While I was growing up and playing football in the backyard, from time to time I would pretend to be at the NFL Draft, but that never included all the technical stuff that goes into being drafted.

First, there was the Standard Representation Agreement, known as the SRA. It's really just the contract between the player and agent. After reading over the one-page document quickly, I signed at the bottom. It had a lot of legal language, but I trusted Jordan.

Although Jordan didn't intend to represent anyone for another year, he called a friend at REP 1 Sports, one of the premiere sports agencies.

As a team, they were going to represent me. In fact, Jordan had been talking with them for a while about leaving ESPN and becoming an agent with their team. Later he told me that's why he waited to agree to represent me. Because of his lack of experience, he wanted to be sure he had an agreement to work for REP 1 first.

"Why REP 1, Jordan?"

Jordan lit up. "Why them? Other than the fact I have friends there, I believe in the way they do things. They understand athletes. They understand their needs, their interest, and their goals. They understand what it takes to play at the highest level. They know the ability, heart, and sacrifice it takes to make it in the NFL. They get it, and they live it. They are like a family and are driven by the same competitive spirit. They are genuine and well respected in the industry."

I liked what Jordan said about REP 1, and the information on their website was impressive too. After I signed the SRA, it was official. That did it. I was, as they say, signed sealed and delivered. For the first time it felt like I was on my way to the NFL—and I knew I was in good hands.

We drove over to their office and I was blown away.

They had already been working on a game plan for me before I arrived.

I felt special when I walked in. Their office area was cool with several big screen TVs, and even a ping-pong table. Fathead images of players were on the walls, and signed helmets and footballs were everywhere. One wall had a massive bookcase and I recognized a few of my favorite titles, like Mark Batterson's *Chase the Lion* and Andy Andrews' *The Seven Decisions*.

Yes, the REP 1 office was way cool. Everyone was professional, yet very friendly, and comfortable to be around. There was a gym and a workout area with weight machines, ice tubs, and anything an athlete could want. They provided me with a personal trainer and a nutritionist. They helped me prepare for team interviews and all other tests and situations I would face during the process. They provided a plush apartment complete with a king size bed, huge TV, and access to a really nice swimming pool and hot tub. They had everything covered.

The only thing left for me to do was the work.

+ + +

Dad and I stayed in touch by phone. He was doing as well as could be expected. There were times he told me he was working on some new lyrics, since there wasn't much else to do while being locked up. He said the food wasn't great but he was making it.

Jordan and REP 1 kept me busy preparing to enhance my draft status, which was looking pretty good at the time. They repeatedly said there was a higher realm for me. At first I wasn't sure what that meant, so I asked. There was a path for me to be drafted #1, but there was a lot in play, and we had a lot of work to do. Many of the pundits and mock drafts were projecting me to go in the first round of the draft. Some were projecting me as a top-five pick.

Everything started piecing together, and also moving very fast.

Phil Savage, from the Senior Bowl, called to check in and confirm I was set to attend the game. Word had gotten out I had signed with Jordan and that he was now with REP 1 Sports. That seemed to show I was legitimate because Jordan was such a high profile and well-respected analyst at ESPN, along with the fact that REP 1 is one of the most respected agencies in the business.

Phil actually called Jordan first, but because I was there with him at the time, he handed the phone to me.

"Hello." I was a little nervous to take the call.

"Adam?"

"Yes sir, this is Adam."

"Hey, Adam. My name is Phil Savage, and I am the Executive Director of the Senior Bowl in Mobile, Alabama."

"Yes sir. I'm Adam."

I stopped. At that point I felt like an idiot. He had already mentioned my name.

Although I could probably guess what he was thinking, he was a pro and jumped right to the point.

"Adam, we would love for you to represent Lee University and be one of our quarterbacks in the Senior Bowl. Would you be interested in doing that?"

"Yes sir! I certainly would."

"Well, it would be our honor to have you, Adam. You will have the opportunity to practice with and play for an NFL coaching staff and enjoy the beauty and wonderful people of Mobile."

"That would be my honor, sir."

Finally, I had my head on straight and gave solid answers to Mr. Savage.

"I don't know if you know it or not, but I went to school not too far from Lee."

"No sir. I didn't know that."

"I played football and baseball at the University of the South, in Sewanee atop the Cumberland Plateau, so I know the area well. We played Lee a couple of times and the Flames were tough."

"That's a beautiful place, sir."

"Lee's campus is beautiful too, and I know you will make those good people proud playing in the Senior Bowl. I will get all the details to Jordan and we will look forward to seeing you in Mobile."

"Thank you, Mr. Savage. Here's Jordan."

I handed the phone back to Jordan and they discussed what would happen next. The plan was for me to be in Mobile, Alabama, for a week practicing with the South team, which was being coached by the Chicago Bears coaching staff. That was pretty exciting for me. It seemed everything Jordan touched went well.

CHAPTER 13

T he time came and I was off to Mobile.

Jordan dropped me off, along with other players represented by REP 1, at John Wayne Airport in Orange County. We were prepared for the week ahead.

The people at the Senior Bowl impressed me. Everyone was nice, and everything was planned and timed out. Of course we practiced every day that week, but we also did some work in the community. Our group went to a children's hospital and signed footballs and pictures for the kids. One of the guys on our team actually dressed up like a clown and made balloon animals. He was their favorite. I was glad I went.

Leading up to game day I kept hearing about this one defensive end on the other team. His name was Buster Babel. He was 6' 3", 257 pounds, and I heard he could run a 40-yard dash in a quick 4.5 seconds. Much of the discussion centered on his mean streak and how he had two motors that would not stop, one in the way he plays, and the other was his mouth. He was the center of conversation about the North team. The coaches did a great job of deflecting as much of the talk as they could. They told us not to let him pull us out of our game with his actions or his mouth.

I played against several teams with a guy like that, and didn't think much about it. I had always been good about not letting anyone get me out of my game. I wasn't worried about it. I had no clue what was coming.

I started the game. For the first play, I was in the shotgun with trips right, and my outside receiver was assigned a fade route. That just means I was about five yards back from the center when I took the snap, and we had three receivers together on the right side with one guy going deep as fast as he could. There was man coverage on him and I could see he broke free early. Pass protection was great for me and I was able to step up in the pocket and get the ball downfield to him in stride. The pass and catch were perfect and we scored.

After I threw the ball, Buster, the defensive end everyone was concerned about, hit me late. There was absolutely no question about the flag the ref threw for roughing the passer. I took the hit alright, but it was what he said before he got up that stuck with me and for the first time another player was starting to get inside my head.

He snarled, "I'm going to lock you up like this on every play, just like your daddy's locked up."

I got up and was about to tear into him when my left tackle pulled me back and said, "He's not worth it, bro. That was a perfect pass. He kept going after you threw the ball, and he got the flag. Remember, Coach said to let it go."

"Okay, I will this time."

After we kicked the ball off, our coverage team caused a fumble and recovered it. We had the ball on their 20. We called a run play and I handed the ball off to our tailback. It was a clean handoff, but he fumbled when he was hit by Buster. Fortunately, I saw the ball when it started to come out and was able to get to it before anyone. There was a pile of people on me, and I was holding on to the ball as if it were my life. There were some dirty deeds, to put it mildly, going at the bottom of that pile. One guy tried to drive his finger into my eye, and I really thought my eyeball was about to pop out. It didn't, and I held on to the football.

As the refs pulled people off the pile, the last one on top of me was Buster. As he was getting up, he pushed me and said, "I am your worst nightmare punk. Just call me Buster the Tornado!"

That was it. He had crossed a line, and there was no going back. At the time, I was convinced he was referring to the tornado that took my mom's life. He insulted my dad the first time, and just brought my late mom into the game. That's when I blew up.

I took my helmet off, which of course, was a penalty against me and not very smart. Then I tore into him as if I were going to rip his heart right out of his chest. I grabbed his facemask and pulled him to the ground. Then I got on top of him and just started pounding. It took two guys and a referee to pull me off him.

As my teammates pulled me away, trainers were already on the field checking on Buster. He actually missed the rest of the game.

The guys were taking me to the sideline, and I was fighting every step of the way! I had lost control. I wasn't finished with Buster. Fortunately, they overpowered me, and took me off the field. As they were letting go, I pushed them away and started to run back onto the field. They caught me and pulled me back to the sideline. By this time, Buster had been helped off the field.

A few other teammates met us at the sideline asking if they could help. I was tossed from the game, which made things worse. I pushed the guys away, not realizing one of them was our head coach.

The only thing to do was to run to the locker room and change. One of the assistant coaches caught up with me to make sure I was okay and to let me know I had pushed the Head Coach. Of course I hadn't seen him, and that angered me even more about the whole situation. Things looked pretty bleak for me at that point. There was a security guard standing at the door preventing a couple of reporters from coming in.

I took a shower and changed, which gave me a little more time to calm down. I was then able to tell the assistant coach what happened and what Buster had said to me. He didn't agree with my reaction on the field, and there was no going back. He did tell me what Buster said could upset anyone.

The next morning, I caught a shuttle to the airport with a few of the other Senior Bowl players. The flight back to California seemed to take forever. After we landed, I made my way to baggage claim and saw Jordan waiting for me.

He was not happy with me.

CHAPTER 14

I was prepared to face what I expected would be a severe scolding. But I was wrong. Jordan had a way of letting me know what I did was disappointing to him without berating me. That's just another reason why I wanted him to be my agent.

"So, Adam. Do you want to tell me what happened in Mobile?"

"No sir. But I will."

"Good. But let's not do it here. Let's get back to the office."

After a short, quiet drive, we were there. We walked into Jordan's office, which was already set up at REP 1. He didn't sit behind his desk as an authoritative figure, but rather sat with me at a corner sectional in his office.

"Adam, I have spoken with Phil Savage and some of your coaches at the Senior Bowl, including the Head Coach."

"I didn't mean to push him, Jordan."

"He knows that, but this situation could have a negative impact on your opportunity in the draft. I've spoken with our team here at REP 1, and we are totally committed to you, but this is going to be more than just a 48-hour news story. You can pull out of this if you really want to. It's just going to take a lot of work."

"Being an NFL quarterback has been a life-long dream of mine, Jordan. I know I've said some different things since my dad was arrested, but this is what I want to do. I believe this is what I was born to do. I not only want to be drafted, I want to be an elite quarterback in the NFL."

"Okay, then we are going to treat you like an elite quarterback, and from now on, you have to display the demeanor and mental strength of an elite quarterback."

"I wouldn't expect anything less, Jordan. I know I keep saying it, but that's just another reason I wanted you to be my agent."

"It's going to get rough, Adam. You are going to hear things in the media that could hurt. They aren't doing it to hurt you, they are just doing their job. Sometimes people get a little carried away and take things too far."

"But it was just this one time. And you should've heard what he said to me! About my mom even!"

Jordan looked straight at me. "Adam, there are people sitting in jail because of something they just did one time. You can't look at it like that. The NFL is an organization dating back to 1920. It's not just a football league, it's a family of owners, coaches, players, and administrators committed to excellence in the game, protecting the NFL Shield and bringing first class entertainment to people around the world. Being a part of that group, especially being an elite quarterback, means you are a cut above. That's why the spotlight is going to be on you even more now. To the average fan, you came out of nowhere to win the Heisman. Some may have remembered your recruitment to play college ball, but not as many as you might think. Since winning the Heisman, you have been the talk of the football world. People were just beginning to learn more about you as a player and a person. They don't really know you, so they have to go on a very limited amount of knowledge. The same goes for most of the media. So we are dealing with that, which is something known as the recency bias."

"Recency bias?"

"It's just the tendency to believe that most recent trends and actions are the rule and will continue in the future. It's kind of like hanging on to an interception and letting it impact you during the next series. Like I said, most people, including the media, don't know much about you. The most recent thing they know is that you threw your helmet, had a fight with and injured another player, got ejected from the game, pushed your head coach, and disappeared. Can you see how that is going to be tough for us to combat?"

"Yes sir."

"The good news is that it's not who you are, Adam. It's just the current narrative. We have to change that."

"I will do whatever I have to do to change that narrative, Jordan."

"Well, that's not all."

"This would have happened anyway, but we are also going to have to deal with the level of competition you have been playing in college. It's just something to deal with, but it's the least of our concerns right now. Just know, there could be someone out there trying to get recognized who could try to get you off your game and into a contentious conversation or interview. Like I have told you before, the good ones aren't like that. Although there are always one or two in any industry who will do anything to try to be relevant. You have to be on you're A-Game every minute, every day."

Jordan walked over and picked up a blue folder from his desk and brought it to me.

"Let's go over a few things, Adam."

+ + +

It was the Game Plan they had put together for me. We covered my training program, nutrition, personal evaluations, interviews, and my overall brand as a player. I was impressed.

My commitment to him and the process was as high as it could be. I looked at him and said, "Jordan, you have my complete buy-in. I am ready to go."

His response puzzled me at first.

"That's good, Adam, but there is even a higher level."

"I don't understand, a higher level?"

"That's right. Buy-in is good. But being 'souled' out can take your life and your game to another level. It's simply a more extreme commitment."

"Sold out?"

"Yes, and the key to understanding what I mean might be clearer with a little spelling lesson."

I looked at him even more confused.

"If we're talking about S-O-L-D out," he said, "then that's still not enough. It's a commitment, but what I am saying is S-O-U-L-E-D out. You invest not only your time, mind, and body—but also your heart. You own it. It's a commitment that requires everything you have—and I mean *everything*."

Something clicked inside me at that moment. I got it. It hit me that this is what my mom and dad would want.

"I get it now. I am S-O-U-L-E-D out." I spelled it out that time. It's a higher level of commitment. I could feel it. I knew it was time to live it with everything I have inside.

"Great. Now let's get you to the highest pick in the draft you can be, and get you ready to be more valuable to that team than they can afford to pay. Always focus on being more valuable than anyone can pay you. That's what champions do, Adam."

"Let's do it."

From that moment on, I worked harder than anyone. I studied later, woke up earlier, ate right, took care of myself and prepared to the best of my ability. Other than the times I was able to speak with Elizabeth or my dad, I was totally focused on football.

And although Jordan had prepared me, I was still surprised by what happened next.

CHAPTER 15

It started one night with a text from some number I didn't know.

"Did you drop out of the Draft?"

"*What*? Who is this?"

"Alan from school. I just saw something on TV that said your football career was over."

I didn't know anyone from school named Alan, and had no idea how this person got my number. As I remembered what Jordan told me, I realized it could be someone trying to bait me, so I ignored it and blocked the number.

Unless Jordan told me there would be a call coming in which I would need to take for a legitimate interview or from a team, I only answered my phone for calls from Elizabeth, her mom, Jordan and the guys at REP 1, and the county jail where dad was locked up. It was strange having the County Jail in my contacts on my phone, so one day I just changed the name to 'Dad'.

Upon Jordan's suggestion, I also didn't read or respond to texts from anyone else either. I totally stayed off social media including Instagram, Facebook and Twitter. The only thing going out to the public from me went through Jordan first. I can't tell you how much that helped me focus.

Of course, there is no way to be completely shielded from the outside world. From time to time, I would hear something on TV about a mock draft. Many times my name would be mentioned as someone who had all the potential in the world, followed by a lack of high-level competition in college, a dad in jail, and things relating to the incident at the Senior Bowl.

It hurt, but it also served to inspire me to work harder, study more, and prove them wrong. I would show them what Adam Alford was made of.

+ + +

Dad's situation had not improved. Elizabeth's mom, Bethany, had been working hard to get him released, but to no avail. The local D.A. wouldn't budge and the Judge held him without bail. It just didn't make sense. Still, there was nothing for me to do but wait and pray somehow the truth would come out and prove him to be innocent.

My relationship with Elizabeth was strong. We didn't see each other much in person while I was training, but we were on Facetime every night. It wasn't the same as being together, but we stayed close. Jordan and his wife were awesome. They stayed in close communication with Elizabeth's mom and allowed Elizabeth to stay with them over a couple of weekends when her mom paid for her to fly out to see me. That was great. They were totally going the extra mile for me.

My days were full. Along with the workouts and prep time for interviews, we also had board time. That was time when I would be one-on-one with a coach at a white board explaining the offense I ran in college. We discussed everything, including routes and types of defensive coverages I saw. That was pretty intense. It's one thing to run an offense and just go out there and make it happen. It's quite another to go deep in drawing it out on a board and explaining the dynamics of it to someone.

I was making progress. Still, there were no guarantees. Jordan and the team at REP 1 did everything in their power to prepare me for what I was about to experience. I was as ready as I could be.

These teams were making decisions on whom they would invest millions of dollars. My hope was that I could make the right impression so one of these teams would place a strategic bet on me. Jordan believed in me, the other guys at REP 1 believed in me, and I believed in myself, but what really counted is what NFL teams, or at least just one team, believed.

As always, Jordan had a plan.

+ + +

"Here's our game plan, Adam. Of course we are going to focus on everything we've discussed. As I mentioned before, we have to try to change the narrative about you. We both know you aren't normally the guy who made a few bad decisions at the Senior Bowl. So that's where we have to give special attention, especially as we prepare for certain interviews. Before we do that, there are three people I want you to invest some time with, Adam. I have handpicked these guys for a reason. I will set up the time for you to meet with each of them."

"Great. What will we talk about?"

"You will see when you meet with them. What I want you to do is to come back to me after meeting them and tell me the principle you learned from each one and what actions you will take next."

"Let's do it. Who are they?"

"I want you to meet with Coach Ted Tollner, Coach Chuck Pagano, and Akbar Gbajabiamila."

"The *American Ninja Warrior* guy?"

"Yep, that's him."

"Man, I love that show! And Coach Pagano is one of my favorite NFL coaches. I love the Colts, and Coach Tollner is an icon—a genius when it comes to the passing game. When it looked like Steve Young might be playing defense in college, Tollner was the one who gave him a real shot at playing quarterback. I learned all that when Young was inducted into the Hall of Fame."

"You certainly know your football, Adam."

"It's almost all I think about."

"Well, these guys will give you a lot more to think about."

"Thanks, Jordan. I can't wait!"

+ + +

The first guy I met was Akbar. He is a busy guy, co-hosting *American Ninja Warrior* and working as an analyst for NFL Network. I was already a fan, so just getting to meet him was cool.

"Hey, Adam. It's great to meet you."

"It's great to meet you too, Mr. Gbajabiamila."

"You can call me Akbar."

"Thanks, Akbar."

"Jordan asked me to meet with you and share a couple of stories."

"I'm all ears."

"One of the stories he wanted me to share with you is one of the scariest things that has ever happened to me."

"You are 6' 6", 260. I can't imagine you ever being afraid of anything."

"I had the barrel of a gun pressed against my chest by one guy, and three others surrounding me. I was afraid."

"I would be too! Where were you?"

"I had recently purchased a car from a friend of mine. It was a BMW 740Li and it was loaded. It was a $90,000 car. It was a bit of a status symbol, and I thought driving that car let people know I had made it. I can tell you it turned a lot of heads. The problem was that it also turned the heads of four guys who wanted to take it from me."

"Oh, man," I inserted.

"Yeah, so I drove over to a friend's house and was parking the car when I saw these four guys approach. I was thinking they were going to tell me I couldn't park there. The next thing I knew I was lying on the ground as my life flashed in front of me. At that point, the car, the money, and nothing else mattered. The only thing that mattered was my life. Everything else could be replaced."

"I'd feel the same way."

"You see, Adam, people can take things away from you, but there are only a few things which can't be replaced. Those are the things that really matter. My perspective on life changed that day. The police found the car. Someone had stripped the navigation system and some other things out of it, probably around $40,000 worth of damage done. Although I could have replaced it all, I decided not to. I got the car back, then got rid of it about a month later. I decided other things mattered much more than driving a car that would turn heads. I decided who I am mattered, and what I possessed didn't matter at all. Don't get me wrong, I like nice things. I just have a different perspective about it."

"Things that can be replaced must never take precedence over what really matters."

"That's right, Adam. Focus first on who you are and why you are here. Everything else follows. Everything."

"You mean my purpose?"

"Yes, your purpose. You might be thinking your purpose is to play pro football, but I believe it's something greater than that. Football may just be the vehicle you have right now to live out your purpose and pave the way for an exciting future after football. Think about it like this, when your football career is over, is your life over?"

"I hope not."

"Right. Someday you won't be playing football anymore, but you can continue to live out your purpose. What I am about to share with you may be one of the most important lessons you will ever learn. I'm not saying this because I believe I am so smart and know all the secrets of life. I am saying it out of a heart of conviction because I know it's true; it ties in to the second story Jordan wanted me to share with you."

"What's that?"

"It's the story of me and the NFL Draft."

"Which team drafted you?"

"That's just it. I wasn't drafted. I'll never forget the 2003 NFL Draft when I was at J.R. Tolver's house. He was a teammate and friend of mine at San Diego State. He was a great receiver, and was drafted in the 5th Round. Pick after pick, I watched as the available spots dwindled one by one until there were only 5 picks left. I watched my dream fade away one team and one pick at a time. I remember walking out of the house because I just couldn't stand it anymore. With tears in my eyes, I wandered around walking the streets wondering what would become of my life. The Draft ended and I wasn't drafted. It was over."

"But you did play in the NFL. I know you retired as an Oakland Raider."

"You're right, Adam. You see, when I was driving that BMW, I thought I had made it, but it wasn't the car that defined me. When I wasn't selected in the draft, I thought it was over, but it wasn't over. As long as you have a breath, it's never over. After the draft ended my agent, Bruce, called me and asked what I thought about playing for the Silver and Black. When he said that, I knew instantly he was talking about the Raiders."

"So you were an Undrafted Free Agent?"

"That's right. On the final day of cuts, I hid out in the auxiliary locker room just to keep my dream alive as long as I could. I knew that if I couldn't be found, no one could ask me to bring my playbook to the coach's office."

"That would mean you were being cut."

"That's exactly what that would mean. Nobody wants to hear that, so I hid. At a certain point I had to go out onto the practice field. I knew that if they were looking for me, that's when they would tell me. It was time for me to face the music. I ran out onto the field and Bill Romanowski, a guy who was in his 16th year of playing in the NFL, popped me on my butt and said, 'Congratulations, you made it.' I looked at him and said, 'Not yet.' I still had three minutes until the horn sounded. Those three minutes seemed like an eternity, but it passed and I heard the horn sound, which meant practice had started and I was not cut. I realized I had made it. I was in the NFL. Practice started and tears were coming down my face because my dream of playing in the NFL was real."

He paused and looked into my eyes, letting his story sink in.

"You see, Adam, tears were flowing when I thought it was over, and tears were also flowing when I realized I was living my dream. I gave it everything I had, and then one day, my playing days in the NFL were over. It was time for the next phase of my life. The NFL had selected me to attend Broadcast Boot Camp, and I knew that's what was next for me. You see, one thing leads to another. Had I given up on football because I wasn't drafted, I would have never made the team with Oakland. Also, had I not given it my best, I wouldn't have stayed as long as I did and been able to meet the people I met. Had that not happened, I wouldn't have attended Broadcast Boot Camp and been able to do what I do today. Adam, if all that had not happened, you wouldn't call me the *American Ninja Warrior* guy."

"Oh, you heard about me calling you that?"

"Do you believe for one minute that Jordan wouldn't tell me that?" We both laughed.

"Thank you, Akbar."

"Just remember, be sure you know what defines you, Adam. It isn't a car, a house, the clothes you wear, what team you play for, or all the accolades you might receive. It's not about what anyone else thinks or says about you. It's about who you are and what you do with it. That's a gift. It's about your purpose."

"My purpose."

"That's right, Adam. Purpose begins to come into focus at the point where desire intersects with potential. I believe we all have purpose. I believe that you will have a desire to fulfill your purpose and that you have the potential to do it. There are a lot of people who want to play in the NFL but don't have the potential, so that can't be part of their purpose. There are also a few with potential, but no desire. They don't need to be there either. It can be tricky. Just because you want to do something, and have the potential to do it, doesn't make it your purpose either. That happens to all of us when we want to do something that isn't good to do. You have to do a heart check and ask yourself three questions: Do I have the potential to make it happen? Do I have the desire to follow through? Based on everything I know, is it the right thing to do?"

I nodded, mentally memorizing each question.

"If the answer to all those questions is YES, that's a good indication you are on the right track. You have to ask those questions all day, every day. The outcome of your life is mostly determined by the choices you make."

+ + +

After soaking in so much from Akbar, I was ready for my next meeting, which was with Ted Tollner. Jordan wanted us to meet at Cal-Poly in San Luis Obispo, CA, so we got up early one morning and made the drive.

He dropped me off near the stadium by what is known as Mustang Memorial Plaza—and I was about to find out why.

"Hello, Coach Tollner. It's an honor to meet you, sir."

"It's a pleasure to meet you too, Adam. Jordan has told me a lot about you. He wanted me to share with you something that happened to me while I was a student playing quarterback here at Cal Poly."

"I would love to hear what you have to say, Coach Tollner."

He ushered me over to a place nearby where we could sit.

"Adam, I was the starting quarterback for the team here in 1960. On October 29th, we played Bowling Green University and lost that game 50-6. That date represents the most devastating loss in the history of Cal Poly, not because of what happened in that game, but because of what happened on our way home. We had a midnight flight scheduled to fly back home from the airport in Toledo, Ohio. We had a short bus ride to the airport. There was a dense fog in the area. We were glad to make it to the airport. After a short wait in the terminal area, we walked onto the tarmac toward the C-46 waiting to fly us home. The fog was so thick we could barely see the plane only a few yards in front of us."

He paused and I leaned in closer to hear what he was about to tell me.

"During the boarding process, wide receiver Curtis Hill, who had become ill on the bumpy outbound flight, asked if he could change seats with me. Because I was a team captain, the pecking order gave me a seat near the front of the plane. Curtis hoped that a seat closer to the front of the plane would provide a smoother ride home. I agreed and we changed seats. I found the seat originally occupied by Curtis and settled in for the long flight home. It would be the shortest flight we would ever take."

I was hanging on to every word he said. Coach Tollner closed his eyes for a moment, took a deep breath and continued.

"After a few minutes, the plane was rolling down the runway toward takeoff. Tragedy struck only seconds after takeoff. We were just over 100 feet in the air when the left engine quit, and the plane slammed into the ground and split into two pieces. Everyone in my row and the rows behind me survived. Everyone in front of me, including Curtis, lost their lives that day. It was an unexplainable mystery of mercy that I survived. The only explanation is that it was not my time to go. Today we are sitting just outside of Mustang Memorial Plaza. This is the Memorial for those lives lost that day. Curtis Hill's name is represented as part of the memorial; mine isn't."

"Incredible!" I said. "What a strange twist of fate."

Coach Tollner nodded and said, "That day I realized the importance of the time and position we have in this life. I realized how quickly it could end, and I realized the importance of how I invest my time. I realized any one of us could be a seat change away from something drastically different. I also realized that not everything in life is going to end well. You won't win every game, but you go on. I feel it is my responsibility to do everything I can to make the most of this life. I believe that's what you should do too. That choice is yours alone to make."

I was blown away. His message sounded similar to what Akbar had told me earlier.

"Thank you, Coach Tollner. I will never forget."

+ + +

The next morning, I was ready for my time with Coach Chuck Pagano, the Head Coach of the Indianapolis Colts. Jordan knew he would be in the area so he arranged for us to meet in Orange County. This was a one-on-one meeting with an NFL Coach and I was excited. Of course I knew the Colts would not be considering me in the draft because they were set at the quarterback position. That took some pressure off, but didn't put a dent in the excitement.

"Hello, Coach Pagano, I'm Adam."

I was trying to stand as straight and tall as I could.

"It's good to meet you, Adam."

"I am excited to meet with you, sir."

"The pleasure is mine. Let's get started. Jordan wanted me to share with you my story."

"I've read your book, *Sidelined*, Coach—loved it. Your battle and recovery from cancer really inspired me."

"Thank you, Adam. We put our hearts into writing it. As you may remember from reading the book, becoming a Head Coach in the NFL was a dream of mine, much like your dream to be an NFL Quarterback. Not long after I became the Head Coach of the Indianapolis Colts, I was diagnosed with acute promyelocytic leukemia – known as APL. I was in for the fight of my life, for my life. With great medical care, and God's help, I won that battle."

"Were you afraid?"

"My wife, Tina, and I were stunned. But we knew we had to pray. We knew we had friends who would pray, we knew we had to fight, and we knew we had hope. We knew my diagnosis, and we knew what we had inside. You see, Adam, circumstances don't make you, they reveal you…"

I interrupted. "Hold on, Coach. I want to write that down."

He smiled and waited as I quickly wrote what he had just said to me. Then he continued.

"You can't always count on life – or football games – to go as you expect. You have to focus on the process, do the work, take it one day at a time and stick to it. You know this, Adam. In football, we are given a schedule that tells us when we have game days during the season and where we will play. We add practice days, travel days, and off days. We aren't handed a schedule for our life, but we are basically handed a calendar. The days on that calendar represent days you have here on earth. It's not about the circumstances you come up against. We all have circumstances. You don't live in circumstances, you live and play through them. You live in vision. You have to know your vision, and then you have to do everything you can do to live it. That choice can only be made by you."

I had heard three powerful messages from three very influential people.

"Coach, did Jordan give you guys a script?"

"A script?"

"Well, I have spoken with Akbar Gbajabiamila, Coach Ted Tollner, and now you. All three of you, in different words, have told me a message very similar to what Jordan has been saying. Something I must need to hear."

"Jordan just told me to tell you the truth. If we're all on the same page, it's because we've each learned what matters most in life."

"I believe it, Coach."

"Okay, so now that you believe it, what are you going to do with it?"

"The first thing I am going to do is what Jordan asked me to do. He asked me to come back to him after meeting with you guys and tell him the principles I learned from each one of you and what actions I will take next. So that's my next step."

"That's great, Adam. Now let's go back to my original question. What are you going to do with it? What specific actions will you take next? What are you going to tell Jordan?"

"Although I'm sure I will think of more later, here's my list for now:

- Share with Jordan my purpose, which is to have uncommon influence on people on and off the field. By uncommon influence, I mean influence that can change the trajectory of someone's life.

- Make the proclamation every day that: Every day is Game Day. I will give my best every minute of every day to live out my purpose. Every moment of every minute of every hour of every day counts. It's my job to make the most of every one of them.
- Continue to keep a journal.
- Go through the Game Plan material Jordan gave me, which includes: reading the books *Uncommon Influence*, *Living Forward*, and *Chase the Lion*, and joining www.SouledOutElite.com to help me close the gaps between where I am and where I want to be in several areas in my life.
- Develop my own personal Life Plan based on the format given in the Living Forward book.
- Focus on excellence in everything, not just football.
- Make things right with Buster, the defensive end I fought with at the Senior Bowl."

"That's a great start, Adam. If you do all of that, I am very confident your future in the NFL will be bright."

I thanked him for his time and wise counsel, and we shook hands.

I had a lot to think about.

+ + +

I could sense something significant had changed inside of me after investing time with these three great men. I really appreciated Jordan putting us together. These men had uncommon influence on me. What they said had changed the trajectory of my life, and probably the trajectory of where I would be picked in the draft. I had work to do on the outside, but the most important change had happened on the inside.

The next day, back at REP 1's office complex, Jordan shared they had a field trip planned for us that day. We were going to CHOC, which stands for the Children's Hospital of Orange County. I knew it would be a special day, and it was.

I learned a lot that day. We brought tall containers called "Joy Jars" filled with small toys to the kids at the hospital who were battling life-threatening illnesses and watched their faces light up. We took pictures with the kids and just hung out for a while with them and let them know they are special. Their smiles did something for me. I still have a picture from that day on my phone and I always will, because I always want to remember that experience.

Being with the kids put everything I was told earlier into perspective. It made me think deeper about my purpose. I learned about Jessie Rees and how, as a 12 year-old fighting cancer, she inspired other kids fighting childhood cancer to Never Ever Give Up. It was Jessie's vision to create toy jars for other children. This experience taught me that we all have the ability and responsibility to help others and give back. The Jessie Rees Foundation, NEGU, continues her vision and legacy today.

The next couple of days, after each workout, I autographed stickers that would be placed on collectable player cards for the companies Upper Deck and Panini for around $25 per card. They sell the cards to fans. I signed a little over 20,000 stickers for cards. By that time, it wasn't about the money. Of course there were some cool things I wanted like a Ford F-150 and a Breitling watch like the one I wore at the Heisman Award ceremony. I had been looking at that watch online for a while. I knew it would be okay to get some cool stuff at the right time.

CHAPTER 16

The process of NFL teams making the decision to draft a specific player is intense. I always thought if I were good enough on the field, I would be drafted. I thought the better I was during a game, the higher I could be drafted. It's just not that simple. Although talent is very important (if you don't have enough talent, you won't get drafted), so many other things such as character, leadership ability, and cognitive skill sets, as well as height, weight, and speed are considered heavily. Each draft pick is a major investment on the financial side, as well as for the future of the team.

I have talent. In spite of the fact my school didn't get a lot of media attention, I won the coveted Heisman. It had been well documented that I seemed to have what it takes to be a franchise quarterback. People were believing I could play and lead in such a way as to help my team consistently win in the NFL, that is until I did what I did at the Senior Bowl. With recent negative stories about players in the NFL, off-field conduct has become a bigger factor to consider in the Draft.

That one incident caused many in the media, and inside NFL teams, to begin to question my potential. Some in the media even questioned whether I should be drafted. Because of that one incident, everything was being questioned about me. As Jordan told me earlier, it was going to be an uphill battle, but I was ready. Having a clear purpose changes everything.

My days consisted of physical, mental, and emotional training. I read every book Jordan suggested. I wrote in my journal every day, being careful to capture every quote and thought that resonated with me. Drafted or not, I was trying to become a better man.

Dad and I stayed connected and, although I couldn't quite put my finger on it, I could tell something good was going on with him. It was almost like he was going through the same growing process. I didn't know Jordan was taking him through a similar game plan which had been approved by the county while he was in jail. He was still locked up, still charged with murder and waiting for trial, but something significant was different about his language. I was actually encouraged after speaking with him on the phone each week.

I was working hard, and I loved every minute of it.

+ + +

Work isn't hard when you are chasing something important to you. My purpose was now bigger than the NFL Draft. Don't get me wrong, there was no doubt playing quarterback was part of my purpose in life, but it was just a part. I became so focused on not just being able to convince an NFL team to draft me, but I was focused on becoming the absolute best quarterback I could become.

As I read in the book *Every Day is Game Day*, I realized there were two types of potential, Known and Unknown. Prior to the incident at the Senior Bowl, everyone was talking about my Known Potential. My footwork had been analyzed (maybe over analyzed), and my release of the ball had been studied under a microscope. There had been a lot of discussion about what other people called my perfect touch in getting the ball to the right place at the right time, whether it was a screen or the deep ball. Some call this "throwing a receiver open." It was my "unknown potential", or what people believed I could accomplish, which I had not yet proven. This led people to talk about my having a high ceiling in the game.

My next opportunity to show off my abilities was at the NFL Combine. It takes place in February, in Indianapolis at Lucas Oil Stadium, home of the Indianapolis Colts. Imagine an intense four-day job interview. Top executives, coaching staffs, player personnel staffs, and medical personnel from all 32 NFL teams are there to evaluate a little over three hundred college football players who were invited to attend. I had worked out physically, mentally, and felt emotionally sound.

Although I knew there would be some tough questions for me, I was ready and excited. Almost everything which could be recorded about me, including the size of my hands, was measured and documented on my stat sheet:

Height	6'3"
Weight	222.4 lbs.
Arm Length	32 in
Hand	9 7/8 in
40 Time	4.52 sec
3 Cone Drill	6.87 sec
Vertical Jump	36.0 in
Short Shuttle	4.08 sec
Broad Jump	10 feet

Many of the analysts were talking about my strengths along with what they perceived were my two major weaknesses. One sports blog in particular summed it all up:

Alford's Strengths:
- A quick-twitch quarterback with rare straight-line speed
- Keen sense of where trouble lurks and almost never gets baited into a dangerous throw
- Able to make off balance, difficult throws
- Silky smooth when asked to roll out and delivers on time with sound mechanics
- Can uncork throws quickly and without resetting feet when necessary
- Can climb the pocket and deliver strikes when he trusts the edges of his protection
- Strong family ties with his dad

Alford's Weaknesses:
- Incident at the Senior Bowl
- Competition in college is questionable

Although it wasn't a weakness, my dad's being in jail at the time was considered a negative factor.

My "known potential" in terms of size and mechanics as a quarterback was solid. There were no real concerns there. My "unknown potential" in terms of improving as a quarterback, had been discussed as my having a high ceiling.

My "unknown potential" in terms of leadership and emotional stability were in question because of that one incident. Was that fair? At one time I would have said absolutely not. After the three meetings with the guys who had uncommon influence on me, I can say that was absolutely fair. What I did at the Senior Bowl was wrong.

The biggest question for NFL teams was how much to factor that into their evaluation of me.

+ + +

I realized everything I did, or didn't do, in the past affected where I was today. I knew there was nothing I could do about the past, other than learn from it. There was nothing I could do about the future, other than plan for it. Today is the only day I have to take action; and everything I do or don't do today will affect where I will be tomorrow.

It was clear there were things I had total control over, and things I had little or no control over. I was determined to control the things I could control with excellence, and either influence or adjust to the things I could not control.

I couldn't control what other people thought or said about me, but I could influence their thinking, which in turn would influence their words. In the end, I was responsible for me.

The biggest question I had for myself, I answered.

I knew everything was going to be okay, drafted or not. The work I had to do was to go deeper in living out my purpose to have uncommon influence on other people, in order to do something to change the trajectory of their life in a good way. I finally realized every day truly is game day, and that every moment of every minute of every hour of every day counts.

I knew it was up to me to make the most of every one of them.

+ + +

As an Analyst at ESPN, Jordan had developed a Return on Draft Investment profile to value each quarterback drafted over a period of ten years. This profile was now being used by several teams to help determine who to draft to fill their quarterback needs. The formula consisted of games played, completion percentage, yards per attempt, TD / interception ratio, height, hand size, EQ, FQ (which is Football Quotient), and a couple of other results from the NFL Combine. The respect and uncommon influence he has in the NFL probably caused some teams to take a second look at me just because he was my agent. He had become somewhat of a guru in terms of assessing current and potential NFL quarterbacks.

As I walked onto the Lucas Oil field at the Combine, I had the same feeling I had in New York at the Heisman Award Ceremony, like being in a dream.

I was actually standing on an NFL field. I looked up at the stands and considered that I was one step closer to thousands of fans watching me play the game I loved so much. It hit me that there would be millions more watching on TV. There was a time when that thought would lead me to think about fortune and fame.

Not this day. Instead I thought about the awesome opportunity to be a positive influence to the team that would draft me, their fans, the NFL itself, and fans around the world. I wanted to be an example parents would want their kids to look up to. I wanted to be a role model in the purest sense. That reminded me about a study titled *PROVEN PLAYER*, which a guy named John Powell taught us at an FCA meeting while I was playing football at Lee. Each letter stood for something different. When it's all put together it defines what it means to be a proven player, and that's what I wanted to be.

I couldn't stop thinking about the opportunity to have uncommon influence on my future teammates and fellow players on other NFL teams. I had visions of being a leader in the locker room. For these reasons, I wanted to be an NFL quarterback more than ever.

+ + +

As good as it was going for me at the time, there was a moment of truth about to confront me in front of the Crowne Plaza where all the players attending the Combine were staying. If it weren't real already, it was about to get real quickly. Without warning, I was standing face to face with Buster Babel, the defensive end with whom I had the altercation at the Senior Bowl.

But I had already committed to make things right with Buster, and here was my chance. Although I had no idea how he would react, it didn't matter. I had something to do. It wasn't about Buster; it was about me.

"Hey, man. I'm sorry for what happened at the Senior Bowl."

"For what?"

"For what happened on the field. I know what you said, although it was personal, you were just trying to get inside my head, and you did. It hurt when you said something about my dad being locked up, and I got mad. Then you said something about the tornado that killed my mom, and I lost it."

"The tornado that killed your mom?"

I could tell he had no clue.

What I was about to say was so tough, and I had trouble getting the words out. I looked down at the ground and said,

"After the fumble recovery, as you were getting up, you said, 'I'm your worst nightmare punk. Just call me Buster the Tornado.' I thought you were referring to my nightmare about the tornado that took my mom's life when I was ten years old."

When I looked back up at him, his expression had drastically changed. He started tearing up.

"Bro, I had no idea about your mom. I've always been called Buster the Tornado. It's been my calling card since I was a kid. That's just what I say many times to get in a quarterback's head. I had no idea."

"You didn't know?"

"I had no clue, Adam. The only reason I said anything about your dad was because my dad has been locked up most of my life. I know how it feels when other people talk about it. I was just trying to get inside your head with that statement because I know how it affects me. Of all people, I should have known better than to cross that line. There are other ways to get inside somebody's head. Will you forgive me?"

"Yes. Yes, I will. And you'll forgive me?"

"Of course, man. We're good. But it won't stop me from slamming your little quarterback butt on the ground the next time I get a chance on the field." He wiped his eye with his hand and smiled.

I looked at him and said, "I wouldn't expect anything less from you, Buster. But you're going to have to catch me first."

We embraced, and I could hear the shutter click of a camera.

Apparently, as we were speaking, reporters had gathered around us. Our conversation was so intense, neither of us had noticed.

Reporters pressed in asking questions about what was said. I had to go take a test.

Buster said, "Go on, Adam, I got this."

Not being one to be camera shy, Buster told the whole story.

The news of that exchange was as far reaching as the incident at the Senior Bowl. Twitter lit up. At one point, #TheEmbrace was actually trending. Instagram was blowing up too. The press was all over it. This became the story of the day; for whatever reason, it made ESPN's Top Ten Plays of the Day. It was actually #1.

The only thing that mattered to me was the fact that I was able to cross that one off my list of things to do. Although making peace with Buster was very important to me, I really thought it would just be a big deal in the media for a day or so and, like everything else, pass away in the 48-hour news cycle. I was wrong. It came up in every interview while I was at the Combine, and every team specific interview afterward. Neither Buster nor I intended for our chance encounter to be newsworthy. We were just two guys working something out between us.

Next on my schedule was for me to be in front of the media. I had an opening statement to give and then open Q&A. It was the day after the chance-meeting with Buster.

It had been just about three weeks between what had been well documented as "The Incident" and "The Embrace." I knew I needed to address it but didn't want to create another media circus around it.

Jordan was in town and we were able to talk in the restaurant near the lobby of the Crowne Plaza. I had written my opening remarks and asked him to read over them and let me know what he thought. After reading my remarks, he just smiled and said, "That's uncommon, Adam."

That's all I needed to hear.

+ + +

In a flash I was standing in front of a rather large contingent of sports media people, sometimes referred to in the business as a *scrum*. Cameras and lights were all aimed at me. I recognized some reporters from personal encounters and some from seeing them on TV. There were so many there, and they were all focused on me. It could have been pretty scary, but I just took a deep breath, remembered my purpose, and began to speak:

"I want to first thank the NFL for inviting me to the Combine. I'll never forget the first NFL game I saw as a child. It was the Super Bowl. I was barely old enough to know anything about either team, but I fell in love with the game. During the first half, I was pulling for one team, but because of the influence of a friend at the time, I changed that short-term allegiance during halftime. The team I settled on lost that day, but it didn't matter to me. I became a fan, not only of that one team, but also of the game."

I smiled and waited a beat before continuing. "The next day I told my dad I wanted a football and that I was going to be an NFL quarterback one day. That was a long time ago. Although there have been some challenges and devastating losses along the way, some caused by me, and some completely out of my control; I stand here ready to serve. My potential has been analyzed and discussed among many of you. My "known potential" is documented. What I have done is what I have proved I can do; I believe there is more. I believe there is "unknown potential" that is yet to be tapped. I believe with my commitment and coaching I can become stronger, faster, and smarter in a way so I may become very successful as a quarterback."

From there I described how my agent Jordan Cassidy had helped me with a Game Plan to discover my purpose and to better understand the concept of Unknown Potential. I relayed how, during the course of that period of discovery and understanding, I committed to seven promises. I had written them out, printed a copy, and shared them that day:

1. I promise myself I will do my best to pursue the fulfillment of my purpose until the day I die.
2. To my family, I promise to continue to love you and try to do my part to make your life better.
3. To whichever team selects me, I promise to be the best possible quarterback I can be, to continue to learn, grow, and improve in such a way that their Return On Draft Investment (RODI) will be as high as I can possibly achieve.
4. To my future teammates, I promise to do my best to help you be at your highest level on and off the field.
5. To the community and fans of the team that selects me, I promise to represent you in a way that will make you proud your team selected me.

6. To the NFL, I promise to protect the Shield and represent you well. The NFL is not just an institution in the entertainment industry. It's a family of 32 teams and the people representing those teams. There is a rich history to be proud of and what I believe to be a phenomenal future ahead.

7. Finally, to you members of the media, I know your job is tough. I know there will be times I can share things with you and times I can't. I want you to know that I understand you have a tough job. I grew up watching and listening to you. What you did played a significant role in my wanting to be an NFL quarterback. My promise to you is to respect your role and to be available and open to you, to the extent I can.

+ + +

It was quiet for longer than usual after the opening remarks at a Combine press conference. I hoped they were actually thinking about what I just said. But then the questions began to flow.

"Adam, what changed you between the incident at the Senior Bowl and today?"

"Thank you for your question. I am not going to make any excuses for my actions at the Senior Bowl. What I did was wrong. I have apologized to Mr. Savage with the Senior Bowl and the coach I pushed. That's the only time I have ever been ejected from a game, the only time I have taken my helmet off while on the field, or hit another player. It's the only time I have ever walked into the locker room during game play other than one time when I was injured. I believe the incident was an outlier and not representative of who I am as a quarterback, or as a man."

I made eye contact with the reporter who had asked the question before continuing. "However, what happened that day happened. It clearly showed I had the propensity to take those actions, and that concerned me. I believe it was because, at the time, I had not understood my purpose in life. I have invested a lot of time thinking over the last few weeks, and I discovered my purpose. I can tell you that the type of behavior at the Senior Bowl will never happen again."

Another reporter had a follow-up question.

"So what is this purpose which drives you now, Adam?"

"As I mentioned in my remarks earlier, my purpose is to have uncommon influence on as many people as I can, on and off the field."

One of the event coordinators stepped in and made the group aware we had time for two more questions.

Another reporter asked: "Over the past couple of weeks, there has been a lot of talk about you possibly not being drafted at all. If that's the case, what will you do?"

"Thank you for that question. There is no doubt in my mind, that if I am not drafted, I will focus on making a team as an undrafted free agent. If that happens, I will be just as committed as I mentioned earlier. The promises will remain the same. If for some reason I don't make the cut for a team, I will find another way to live out my purpose. It's that simple."

The last question was from the back of the room: "After the famous embrace with Buster, he shared with us what had been said between the two of you. Does that clear up everything between you?"

"Buster and I are good, although he did say that wouldn't stop him from slamming my little quarterback butt on the ground during a game. In response to that, I told him he would have to catch me first."

Everyone laughed and it was time for the next player up.

+ + +

The Combine was like a blur to me because we were always moving around to the next event, mental test, or physical test. From lots of time at the hospital having X-Rays and MRI's, to waking up for a urine test at 5:00 AM, we were on the go. For me, it was a combination of enjoying the process while being intensely focused. I met a lot of cool people there.

One person was Ken Dorsey, who is the quarterbacks' coach for Cam Newton with the Carolina Panthers. If anybody knew what it took to be a big-time quarterback, it was him. I saw him at the train station next to the Crowne Plaza where there were a lot of informal interviews being conducted with coaches and other NFL personnel.

I knew they weren't looking for a quarterback, but I was happy I had a chance to interview with him.

"Coach Dorsey, my name is—"

"—Adam Alford. I've watched a lot of film of you playing. It was not because we are looking for a quarterback, but because I really like your style. You know, if we didn't have Cam, we might be talking about you possibly being a Panther."

I had no idea he knew my name! "Thank you, sir. Is there any advice you would be open to give me about anything to do with my play, or anything?"

"You know, Adam, just relax and be yourself. I just saw the interview you did for the media and you killed it. It seemed like it came straight from your heart."

"I had some thoughts on paper, but it was all from the heart, Coach."

"That's great. I really liked that you were not like a robot going through the motions just trying to impress people. Stay that way and you will be fine. Some people will try to shake you in interviews, but don't let them. Just remember, teams have a huge decision to make on who they will draft. They just want to be sure that you're their guy."

"Thanks, Coach."

I was glad he gave me that piece of advice. I definitely used it later during some of the interviews. There were some teams who I felt were pushing really hard just to see if I was for real or if they could rattle me, like Buster did at the Senior Bowl. During one interview, one team didn't say anything past the welcome after I walked in; we just sat in silence and watched as they played a video of the four interceptions I threw during my senior season at Lee. That was hard to watch.

After that, we just sat there in complete silence waiting for someone to speak. Finally, someone spoke up, "Uh, what happened with those passes?"

I believe I shocked them by remembering each one in detail. They were surprised when I asked them to play each one again and stop at certain spots during each play. One by one I detailed the mistakes I made, whether it had been misreading the corner, locking in on a receiver, or floating the ball. They were shocked that I had such a grasp of my mistakes. I even shared with them two specific plays which were not interceptions, but could have been had my receiver not taken the ball away from the defender in mid-air. I explained to them that in my analysis of myself, I counted them as interceptions. I then explained how I had been working to reduce the chance for making the same mistakes again.

Someone asked, "What about the third one? Didn't the receiver run the wrong route. Wasn't that one his fault?"

"Sir, I should not have thrown the ball. I should have known the way he was fading out of the route early on that something was wrong. The interception was my fault."

It sounded like someone under their breath asked, "Is he for real?"

Someone else chimed in, "Let's move on to the next question."

Because of my preparation, the interviews were easy to me.

+ + +

Another guy I met while walking on the sidewalk in Indianapolis was John Schneider, the General Manager for the Seattle Seahawks. I had seen him on one episode of *The League*. The episode I saw him in was a funny scene about the Seahawks drafting of Tyler Lockett. He seemed like an approachable guy. Although I was certain they weren't going to draft a quarterback anywhere high in the draft, I wanted to meet this guy.

"Mr. Schneider?"

"Hello, Adam. Call me John." These guys are on top of things.

"Mr. Schneider, I mean John, I loved the episode on *The League* where you drafted Tyler Lockett. I guess some crazy stuff happens on Draft Day."

"You wouldn't believe me if I told you, Adam. It can be a beautiful mess."

"It has been already."

"Good luck in the draft, Adam."

"Thank you, Mr. Schneider."

"You mean John?"

"Oh, yes sir. John."

We shook hands and walked away in different directions.

It was great to be meeting people I had only heard about or seen on TV.

CHAPTER 17

A fter a positive week at the Combine, next up for me was two more weeks of pouring blood, sweat, and tears into my workouts and mental preparation for my Pro Day. I was working hard and missing Elizabeth and my dad. Every time I spoke with Elizabeth, she bugged me about downloading an app called KLOVE Radio. She said it was positive and encouraging. She was right. That app helped me remain focused.

My Pro Day was held at Lee University. It's another time people from NFL teams can take a look at players they are considering. Sometimes they are there to see how players interact with their teammates and coaches; sometimes they are there to look at something specific. Sometimes they are there because they are on the fence about a player and looking for something to move them to one side or the other.

I did not take my foot off the accelerator after the Combine. I was working harder than ever. I was ready for, and excited about, my Pro

Day. Bigger schools usually have several athletes to be observed during their Pro Day. At Lee, there was just me and a couple of others.

I didn't do any of the measured events because I had solid results at the Combine. I just watched the other guys and cheered them on. After they finished, it was time for me to throw. After discussing it with Jordan, I decided to use my own receivers who were at Lee with me. Those were the guys I threw passes to all year, and I knew they wanted to be involved with the process. It was a Win/Win to have them involved. I threw sixty-five balls in a scripted workout with a variety of receiver routes that went very well. One coach from a bad weather city poured water all over the ball and asked me to throw a few more passes. All but one were on the money.

Many teams wanted time to talk with our coaching staff about me. At times it was a little strange for me; I was the only one at the school being considered to go high in the draft and knew almost every conversation that day was focused on me. I saw some people standing on the sideline speaking with Dr. Paul Conn, the President of Lee University. I always enjoyed hearing him speak in Chapel, as well as a couple of times I sat in meetings with him and others during my time at Lee. He also taught my Psychology class. I earned an "A" in that class, so I hoped he had some good things to say about me.

I couldn't control what people were saying, but I could control myself. I just remembered my purpose, and gave it everything I could. All in all, I felt really good about the day. After it was all over, I received a few calls from people who were there, including Dr. Conn, to let me know their conversations went well.

+ + +

After the Pro Day, it was time for individual workouts at my school and meetings alone with a few specific teams without other teams around.

My guys at REP 1 helped me manage the scheduling. The workouts and meetings were held in March at the school.

Then, in April, I had six official visits, which were different, and were held at the specific NFL team's facility. No physical workouts were allowed during those visits. Some of the meetings were intense. There was one team that included a lady sitting in the back of the room. I was never introduced to her. I wondered who she was, but didn't ask. Maybe I should have asked. She didn't say a word, and she didn't take notes. She just stared at me the entire time. At first it bothered me, but I decided that if she weren't going to take part in the interview, I would just ignore she was in the room as I have to ignore trash talk on the field. That interview was odd.

I'll tell you one thing: These NFL teams invest a lot of time and money on their evaluation process for the draft. If all of us evaluated our decisions the way they evaluate draft picks, we would definitely make better choices.

One of my official visits was with the San Francisco 49ers. They were drafting 22nd in the Draft. We discussed not doing that visit because there were other teams to schedule, and we believed I would go higher than 22nd. There was a chance they would trade up for a higher pick in the draft in order to get the quarterback they wanted; we decided to go on the trip.

Their head coach had only been hired recently, but he impressed me with his passion and knowledge of football. He had been an offensive coordinator and quarterbacks coach during his career before joining the Niners. By the end of our meetings and dinner, I really liked this guy and could see myself playing for him. I had already learned that you couldn't fall in love with one team during the draft process.

You had to wait and see who fell in love with you first.

+ + +

Everything was coming together. There was talk about me being back up at the top half of the first round with several NFL teams still looking to draft a quarterback.

Mark Brunell had taken Jordan's place at ESPN. It just made sense; he was a lot like Jordan. He had a great career as a player in the NFL, knew the game inside and out, and was loved by everyone. He had some really nice things to say about me. His analysis of what was going on with me concerning the Draft had me even more fired up.

I wanted to be drafted by almost every team I met with. I was so pumped, I couldn't wait to get drafted and start learning some team's playbook.

Over time something had shifted in the media. I had gone from feeling like a few of them were beating me down, to my story being the Cinderella story of the Draft. It seemed, at this point, many were actually pulling for me.

I didn't let up one bit, in fact, it made me work harder. My life consisted of working out, studying, hanging out with the guys I was training with at REP 1, and taking every opportunity to speak with Elizabeth and Dad.

Being away from Elizabeth was tough. Knowing what Dad was going through was unnerving. Still, I had to press on.

The gym inside the office complex at REP 1 Sports was great. One day while I was just finishing a workout, Jordan came over to the bench and gave me an envelope.

"Adam, this looks like it's from your dad."

I walked over to a chair where I opened the envelope to see what was inside. Sure enough, it was a letter from Dad:

Adam,

I know we talk every chance we get, but I've been meaning to tell you something and I just can't tell you over the phone. I'm just not sure if I could get through it without shedding a few tears. I wanted to tell you in person, but it looks like I'm going to be here for a while.

Several days ago, Dewayne came to visit me. During our visit, he asked me about something specific that happened the night your mom died. He said, just before she passed, he heard her say I love you so much Peter, tell Adam... and he couldn't hear what she said next. Dewayne asked me what she said to me and what she wanted me to tell you. When he asked that question, my mind flashed back to that night. I realized at that moment, although I have always told you how much your mom loved you, I hadn't told you exactly what she said that night.

Adam, after your mom told me she loved me so much, the last words she ever spoke were, 'tell Adam I love him, and tell him to always remember Phil.' Your mom loved you so much Adam, and she never wanted you to forget about Phil.

Today, as I am locked up and accused of something I didn't do, I think about Phil. I can't tell you how much that has helped me over the past several weeks. It will help you too. I know you are working so hard, and are right at the point of getting to live out your lifelong dream to play quarterback in the NFL. Don't forget about Phil.

Love,

Dad

I knew exactly what he was talking about. Phil wasn't a person. Phil was an image that looked a lot like a stick-man on the run. My mom was always coming up with ways to help me remember things. In this case, she had used this image to help me remember Philippians 3:14. We called the stick-man Phil so I could remember the verse was found in Philippians that says: *I press on toward the goal for the prize of the upward call of God in Christ Jesus.* She told me there would be times when I would want to give up and quit, but that I should press on. I had a smile on my face because I realized the truth she taught me was still alive inside of me.

I remembered Coach Jabes had used that verse on a banner while I was at Lee. I knew in my heart it wasn't just a coincidence. I was living it out, pressing on toward the goal to be drafted as an NFL quarterback. It was what I believed God had called me to do at this stage of my life.

CHAPTER 18

I 'll never forget the day the NFL booked my flight to Nashville for the NFL Draft. Seeing my flight information for the first time was exciting. It was evidence of my being one step closer to the big day. I was excited the Draft was going to be held in Nashville for the first time. It was going to be a bit of a homecoming for me because it was being held in my home state. I couldn't wait.

I had done everything in my power to be ready for this day, I went through a lot, and almost lost sight of my dream. I was excited to find out where I would be starting my career.

Although I tried not to get caught up in the hype, I knew there was a lot being discussed in the media about where I would go in the draft. Social media was buzzing with speculation. A few of my college highlights were being shown over and over again on different sports shows. My name seemed to be associated with every team considered to be looking for a quarterback, and even some teams who already had a great quarterback. In most mock drafts, I was projected as going anywhere from the fourth pick to the fifteenth pick in the draft. There were actually a couple of bloggers picking me to go first, but that idea didn't seem to be getting much traction.

Jordan kept me informed about conversations he had with various NFL teams. He told me to take it all in stride and to enjoy the process. From time to time I would catch myself daydreaming about playing for different teams. It really didn't matter to me which team drafted me. I was just thrilled to be on the verge of becoming an NFL quarterback.

Draft week came and we flew to Nashville on Tuesday. Being back home in Tennessee was great. I wanted to drive to Chattanooga to see my dad, but the schedule was full. Dad knew that, and insisted I wait until after I was drafted to make the two-hour drive to see him. He said the next time he saw me, he wanted to know who his new favorite NFL team would be, which of course would be whichever team drafted me. Dad always had a way of making people feel good about stress-filled situations; being locked up had not changed that one bit.

We stayed at the Opryland Hotel, which was like Grand Central Station for the NFL during the week. That place is huge. It was a great place to stay because I didn't have to leave the property for an interview or an event. Although I can't remember how many radio and television interviews I did, there were a lot. The corporate events were fun. I enjoyed the Nike event the most.

It was a bit of a reunion seeing a couple of people I had been with in Indianapolis at the Combine. Jeremiah Clark and I saw each other going and coming from interviews, as well as at the NFLPA and other corporate events. The most fun I had was with Buster.

At one of the events, during a quick conversation we decided to see if we could get another #Something trending. We hatched a plan. Because there were media people and cameras everywhere in the hotel, we decided to give them something to report. After scoping out the best place where we could get the most exposure, we intentionally bumped into each other and just stared each other down like two fighters during weigh in before a fight. The stare was as intense as we could make it.

Sure enough, cameras flashed. After we were sure enough people had captured the moment, we were finally able to give into the smiles we were holding back and recaptured the embrace.

We got what we wanted. #TheStare trended on Twitter. We even scored a vine and it went viral. It's definitely safer to not do things like this.

Later, Jordan told me when he first saw it, it concerned him a bit because he didn't want me trying to be a funny guy at such a serious time. He then told me it ended up being fine. It showed everybody, including the NFL teams who were looking at me, that we had put the entire incident behind us and we were just having some fun.

+ + +

Several teams were still considering me, so things were looking good. Most of them had quarterbacks retiring within the next year or two, and one seemed to need a quarterback in the coming year. It all came down to Jeremiah Clark and me. One NFL Executive with the Eagles said: "It's like vanilla or chocolate, you know? It's like pepperoni pizza or sausage. What do you like better? And that's the best part about this, they're not the same guy. They are different. They are unique in so many ways, and at the same time they both have some really great traits and that gives them a chance. I like vanilla and chocolate."

Some teams were saying, because of the level of competition in college, Jeremiah could be ready to start a bit sooner than I would. Others were saying my ceiling was much higher. They were saying if I could quickly adjust to the speed of the game, I would be fine. With teams potentially looking for a quarterback, and a lot of distance between where we were ranked and the next group of quarterbacks, Jeremiah and

I both hoped we would be selected high in the draft. We just didn't know when and where.

The only thing missing was Dad, and of course my mom, being there with me.

Draft day came. Although I didn't sleep well the night before, I got up early and was ready to go. I was excited that Elizabeth would be there with me. I knew this would be one of the biggest days of my life.

Elizabeth told me her mom would be making the drive to Nashville with her. That morning she called to let me know her mom would not be coming with her. She told Elizabeth something came up and she couldn't make the trip at that time. That bummed me out a bit, but it was really Elizabeth I looked forward to seeing.

She arrived a few hours before the draft. It's hard to describe how I felt when I saw her. She was more beautiful than ever. By the way we acted, people around us probably thought we had not seen or spoken to each other in months.

I couldn't wait for her to see what I had planned to do after I was drafted. During the brief downtime I had, I bought Elizabeth something special from the Mall at Green Hills in Nashville. I was so excited about giving it to her.

When it was time, we made our way to the green room where we would be waiting to see who drafted me, and who drafted the other players in the first round. The green room at the draft is an invitation-only area where each player has a table with their limited number of invited guests.

There we were in the green room. Within the next hour or so, three of my dreams were about to unfold in front of millions.

The first one caught me by complete surprise.

Jordan told me he needed to step away from our table for a moment. I saw him walking out of the room with Gil Brandt, one of the key NFL people at the draft. I wondered what was going on.

When Jordan returned, he wasn't just with Gil. My dad and Bethany were with him! I almost knocked a table over getting to my dad.

"Dad!"

"Adam! I'm free! Bethany proved Roger was at the scene. Lieutenant Max questioned him and he confessed last night! The charges were dropped against me, and thanks to Bethany, I'm a free man!"

"No way? Roger?"

"Yes, Roger."

"Man, that shouldn't surprise me."

"Yeah, she was trying to get a gig at Stick's and Roger was interested in something more. When he saw me leave with her that night, he got jealous and followed us. Apparently, after I left her house, he went in and confronted her and it got more than ugly."

"That's terrible, but I can't believe you are here with me! I can't tell you how happy I am, Dad!" I reached over and hugged Bethany. "Thank you! Thank you! Thank you!"

Jordan chimed in. "Let's get over to the table to wait and see who will be drafting Adam."

I thanked Mr. Brandt for allowing my dad and Bethany to come into the green room at such late notice.

We walked over to the table, took our seats, and waited.

While we were waiting for the draft to begin, I asked Elizabeth's mom to explain more to me about how she got my dad out of jail and the charges against him dropped. She told me something had started bothering her about the evidence a few weeks ago. So she contacted Tommy, the current Attorney General for the County, and took a second look.

As she was looking back over what was found at the scene, she saw that a single contact lens had been listed with everything else. She asked dad if he wore contacts. He said he needed reading glasses but could never bring himself to stick anything in his eyes.

She could not find anything in the report that mentioned Ashley Smith wearing contacts. She questioned some of Ashley's family and friends and everyone said she had never needed glasses. They said she had 20/20 vision. This meant someone else had been there. She then checked to see if a DNA sample could be made from that single contact lens. When it could be, she then ran it against CODIS (Combined DNA Index System). It hit a match; it was Roger, who had a previous conviction for stalking another female.

After hours of intense questioning, Roger confessed to Max that he killed Ashley. He said it was an accident. According to Roger, they were engaged in an argument, he pushed her to the ground, and she hit her head." He shared details unknown to anyone outside of the investigation, and admitted he had lost a contact lens that night. He signed the confession and arrangements were made for my dad to be released from jail the next day.

Bethany was there to pick dad up the next morning in time for them to make it to Nashville for the draft. Not only did she get him out of jail and free from the charges, she brought him a suit and shoes to wear. When she picked him up, he changed at the jail and left with her. It was an answer to my prayers. Now my dad could be here with me on one of the most important nights of my life.

There had been a lot of media buzz in the past few hours because apparently the 49ers had been talking about trading up from their lower position in the draft with a team higher in the draft—and possibly had me in their sights.

+ + +

It was show time! The Commissioner stepped up to the podium, gave his welcoming speech, and announced the 49ers had just traded up for the first pick and were on the clock. Each team has 10 minutes, on the clock, to decide on who they select with that first round pick. Two minutes before the first pick was announced, I received a call on my cell listed as "Unknown Caller."

When I answered, I was greeted by the 49ers head coach and team personnel. My heart skipped a beat.

"Adam, we want you to be our quarterback and lead the 49ers and win a championship with us."

I motioned for Jordan to come listen in on the call, and he just smiled.

"Coach, I don't know what to say! I am so grateful for your trust in me, sir. It's my goal to be the best quarterback in 49ers' history."

"Well, considering the Hall of Famers we have like Joe Montana and Steve Young, that's a tall order to fill, but I believe you have the potential to do it!"

We stayed on the phone until the draft pick was announced by the NFL Commissioner, and it was time for me to step out on stage and get my picture taken with the #1 49ers jersey.

"With the first pick in this year's NFL draft, the San Francisco 49ers have selected…" He paused dramatically. "…Adam Alford from Lee University."

My heart was pounding.

It was time to go on stage.

I grabbed Elizabeth by the hand, and asked her to walk with me to the curtain just off stage. I told her I wanted her to see it live and be close to me.

I was handed a red 49ers hat. I put it on and was given a 49ers jersey as I walked out onto the stage. I was so excited.

After the pictures of me holding the 49ers jersey were taken, I did something nobody expected. I walked over, grabbed Elizabeth's hand, this time pulling her into the spotlight. I reached into my jacket pocket and pulled out a little blue box from Tiffany's. Then I lifted out the black suede ring box, got down on one knee in front of Elizabeth, and opened it.

"Elizabeth, I've been living for this day my entire life. I thought being drafted as an NFL quarterback would be my best day ever. So far, that's true. Only you can make it better. Will you—"

Before I finished, Elizabeth shouted, "Yes!"

I finished anyway. "—marry me?"

She shouted it again. "Yes, Adam, I will marry you!"

I got up. We hugged, added a kiss that may have lasted a bit too long, and walked off the stage with the crowd giving us a standing ovation.

+ + +

As we were leaving, I heard the Commissioner reveal the next pick. "The Chicago Bears have traded up and are on the clock." I was stunned. Within a minute he came back to the podium. "Their pick is in, and the Chicago Bears select Jeremiah Clark from Ole Miss as the second pick of this year's NFL draft."

I wanted to stay backstage long enough to give Jeremiah a high five as he walked on stage to be given his new Bears jersey, but it was time for me to address the media.

During my first interview, I was asked about what would be next.

"I'm heading to San Francisco tomorrow to meet with the 49ers. Then I will head back home to Inspiration, where Elizabeth and I will set a date and start planning our wedding. At some point I want to buy my dad a house in the Bay Area so he will be close to us. I can't wait to get my playbook and get to work becoming the best NFL quarterback I can be."

"Adam? Another question," said the same reporter. "How would you describe your journey to where you are now, the #1 Draft Pick in the National Football League?"

I hesitated and smiled before saying, "Well, I'm not sure I have enough time to describe the wild ride it's taken me to get here. It's had its ups and downs, to say the least."

"Another time then?" the reporter said, adjusting his glasses. "I'd really like to hear the whole story. I think all your new fans would, too."

And that brings us to today. That's how I ended up here, telling you my story.

As we wrapped up our session together and I said goodbye to the reporter, I noticed an email on my phone from the 49ers. Attached was my schedule, with practices, workouts, and team meetings for the next several months. Staring at the schedule, I knew the first pre-season game was about 90 days away in New York. My lifelong dream is now a reality. I am an NFL quarterback. But as I have learned, when you find what you have been looking for, it's not the finish line, it's another starting line. The next chapter has started, time is ticking, and I am living on the clock.

A free eBook edition is available with the purchase of this book.

To claim your free eBook edition:

1. Download the Shelfie app.
2. Write your name in upper case in the box.
3. Use the Shelfie app to submit a photo.
4. Download your eBook to any device.

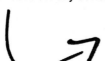

Shelfie

A free eBook edition is available
with the purchase of this print book.

CLEARLY PRINT YOUR NAME ABOVE IN UPPER CASE

Instructions to claim your free eBook edition:
1. Download the Shelfie app for Android or iOS
2. Write your name in **UPPER CASE** above
3. Use the Shelfie app to submit a photo
4. Download your eBook to any device

Print & Digital Together Forever.

Snap a photo

Free eBook

Read anywhere

Morgan James makes all of our titles available
through the Library for All Charity Organizations.

www.LibraryForAll.org